Bestow These Mortal Roots

Copyright © 2025 Barnard Publishing Ltd

All rights reserved

Disclaimer; This is a work of fiction. Unless otherwise indicated, all the names, characters, businesses, places, events, and incidents in this book are either the product of the author's imagination or used in a fictitious manner. Any resemblance to actual persons, living or dead, or actual events is purely coincidental.

Bestow These Mortal Roots © Barnard Publishing Ltd
Call of the Void © Alastair Raper
Breath Upon a Candle Flame © J. Morfa
One's for Sorrow © Imogen Morgan
Supernova © Imogen Morgan
The Doorman © Ben Fitzsimons
Through the Bracken and the Dirt © El Rose

Cover design © Kseniya Savicka (@kseniyasart)
Illustrations © Molly Goodwin (@_taipantattoo_)

ISBN 978-1-7395845-2-8

Barnard Publishing Ltd
Wales

barnard.publishing@gmail.com

www.barnardpublishing.co.uk

Bestow These Mortal Roots

Alastair Raper
J Morfa
Imogen Morgan
Ben Fitzsimmons
El Rose

BARNARD
PUBLISHING LTD.

The Call of the Void	11
Breath Upon A Candle Flame	39
One's For Sorrow	65
Supernova	75
The Doorman	83
Through the Bracken and the Dirt	91

The Call of the Void

Alastair Raper

To all my friends and family who have read and offered feedback on my writing over the years. This wouldn't be possible without you all.

21 December 1923:

Today marks our second month exploring the Amazon rainforest. The rainy season began a few weeks ago and, to be honest, I can hardly say I've noticed the difference. The rainforest is living up to its name and drenching us in torrential downpours almost every day. Even when it doesn't rain, the humidity is such that nothing can dry before the skies reopen on us. And the heat– to keep the mosquitoes at bay, each of us is covered in long cotton clothing that is often soaked with sweat. As you can probably guess we're all feeling a little miserable.

To make things worse, we had to leave Andrew behind this morning. His illness progressed rapidly the night before; we think it's malaria. Luckily, we were able to leave him in the care of the locals. They gave him some sort of tonic made from tree bark and water. I'm not a biologist, so I've no idea what's really in it, but they seemed to think it'd help, so Isaacs allowed it. Amelia stayed behind to look after Andrew; we're all hoping they can re-join us swiftly. It's hard to think our party of seven is now down to five. Redge says the splitting up of our party foreshadows our doom as we head deeper into unexplored territory. His actual words! Our doom! Why a God botherer such as himself even came along on a journey like this is beyond me, but I suppose Isaacs thought we needed some spiritual protection, heading into the unknown as we are. I suppose it helps that he's a talented cartographer and has studied all available maps of the surrounding area more than anyone. As long as he stays up front of the group with his preaching and away from me, I'll be happy.

We trekked all day, as we have for the past four weeks, and I think I'm starting to get used to it. My muscles don't burn the way they used to and I'm getting accustomed to the constant attention, be it from insects, birds, or larger creatures that we can hear but not see. If there's one thing I've learned about the Amazon, it's not a quiet place. If we're passing through waterlogged places, as we are almost every day now, then it's the incessant buzzing of mosquitoes and other insects filling the air. Otherwise, birds of all shapes, colours and sizes compete endlessly with the howls of the monkeys high up in the canopy.

Even now, as I'm writing this from the safety of my hammock's mosquito net, the night is almost as deafening as the day. The ceaseless chirping of cicadas reaches such a level that it could drive a man mad. Indeed, the only comfort I can take in the deafening racket is that it almost drowns out Redge. He has pitched his hammock next to mine and, as he has done every night of this trip– and, I may be correct in saying, every night of his life– is reading aloud from the Bible he carries with him.

If anyone is reading at home upon my return, I do not

wish you to think that I hate the man for his devotion to a higher power– it is simply that I left my God, along with close friends and family, upon the battlefields of France. Fields that, we all agreed over a hearty meal of roasted tortoise, were a hell of a lot quieter than this new green hell we are in. This land is a beautiful one, believe me, but a man could lose his wits entirely if he were to spend too long beneath these misty canopies.

Tomorrow poses the first of the real challenges we're to face in this expedition. Until now we've been moving through relatively well mapped and explored areas, paying visits to friendly tribes to maintain their positive relations with outsiders. Tonight, we're at the final campsite made by myself and Isaacs' good friend Percy Fawcett before he was forced to return to England. Tomorrow, the territory we step into is truly unexplored. I myself do not hold much stock in fanciful tales of missing Amazonian civilisations, but I know at least some of Percy's obsession with it has rubbed off on Isaacs. He keeps talking about the wonders of the lost cities we'll find out there and how wishes Percy could be here with him. We let him talk, as it eats up the miles, but I'm sure he's the only one holding out hope for such a discovery. The rest of us are just in it for the thrill of mapping a new, entirely unexplored region of rainforest.

22 December 1923:

I awoke to the usual rain and, pulling myself from my hammock and, covering myself with my greatcoat, went to see what I could scrounge for my breakfast. Surprisingly I found Martin and Oscar huddled around the embers of last night's fire, trying to coax it back to life in spite of the downpour. They had another tortoise strung up over it. When I asked why it's always tortoises, they simply shrugged and Oscar muttered something about them being easy to catch. With that matter apparently settled, we tucked into some half cooked tortoise meat before we set off into the true unknown.

The terrain seemed intent on taking us downhill, towards the swollen rivers and streams that we are so keen to avoid in this season. We had to detour twice, and more than once a member of our party stepped on what looked to be solid ground only to plunge waist deep or worse into brown murky water. I hope Redge knows where we are, for I've taken so many twists and turns today that I could not have even told you which way we were facing. Occasionally we'd halt so Redge and Isaacs could huddle over the compass and, I assume, make notes on our position before carrying on again. They assured us we were heading north. We continued on like this for hours.

I was walking at the back of the party, ensuring our trail was left clear for any who may attempt to follow when I heard the others shouting. At first, I thought they'd stumbled across a snake– it wouldn't have been the first time– but their cries were of excitement, not alarm. I turned in time to see Isaacs take off running into the trees, with the others soon after him.

Following them, I soon understood their excitement. Ruins. The clear shapes of stone walls lay half buried in the ground; vines hung from larger structures that were formed from immense, precisely cut stones. I drew level with Isaacs, and I could see the look of wonder and joy on his face, on all our faces, at having found some proof of the lost civilisations he'd sought for so long. Even Redge's normally serious face twitched with the hint of a smile.

It was then we realised we weren't the first to have discovered this place. Clearings had been cut in the jungle between these stone structures, and the clear shapes of traditional native huts were visible. They were made from the very trees and foliage that had been cleared to make room for them and we'd slept in many such buildings before during our stays with various local tribes. If anything, Isaacs grew even more excited as we searched the area for the huts' residents, for we had definitely strayed far into their territory and the sooner we introduced ourselves, the better it would go for us. But we found no one. Not a single person had come out to meet us in friendship or in anger. We grew concerned as we searched building after building; Oscar even climbed one of the ruins to try and gain a better vantage point, but there was still no sign of life.

I think I was the last to discover the pit. We'd spread out to search the buildings, and had not seen another member of my party for some time so I made my way to where I thought the centre of the village would be. That was where I found them. They all stood silently staring down into the depths of an immense hole that had formed in the middle of the clearing. It was easily thirty metres across. Its depth I could only guess, for its earthen walls stretched downwards into pitch blackness.

I've always considered myself to be very good with handling heights, but as I joined my fellows in peering over the edge, my stomach flipped violently, and I felt as though the lightest touch of wind would tip me forwards into the blackness. I felt an urge then, felt it in my very soul. The urge to jump into this pit, to surrender everything I had to it. The urge to jump was filling me. I tried to tear my eyes away from the all-encompassing darkness, but no part of my body would respond. At the time I don't think I knew I was leaning forwards; truth be told it felt like the ground itself was tipping, as though offering me up to this waiting hungry void.

Oscar's cry brought me back to my senses and sent me stumbling back from the precipice. I saw him lurch forwards over the edge, and it was only the quick reactions of Isaacs and Redge, who also seemed to have been woken from the same kind of trance as myself, that stopped him being lost to the abyss. I could feel no energy left in my body and I sank to the forest floor as my feet gave way. The others sank with me, their faces looking as tired as I felt, and we sat there at the edge of that void in silence for what felt like hours. None of us wanted to discuss the strange sensation that had enthralled us all. I didn't look at the pit. Whenever I found my eyes glancing its way, I felt the same lurch in my stomach as before and, even though I could no longer see that endless drop, the urge to jump gnawed once again at the back of my mind.

Eventually I noticed that the small glimpses of sky I could make out through the canopy were taking on a darker colour, signalling the coming night. I suggested that we begin to make camp, possibly in one of the seemingly abandoned huts. My voice sounded deafening, but it seemed to bring everyone truly back to the present and almost as one we began the process of setting up our beds for the night.

Not one of us felt hungry, and within the hour we were all in bed. During that hour, I tried to get an impression of how my companions were feeling. I'm sure we all felt the strange desire to jump, but I wonder– do they still feel it as I do, digging away in the back of their heads, drawing their thoughts even now back to that pit and the endless void it contains? As I think back to those moments when we stared into the pit, I become even more unnerved. Not of how close our party came to losing a member to its depths, but of how silent it was. I remarked how my voice seemed deafening when I suggested we set up our camp, and it had been, as, for the first time on our long journey, the jungle was silent. There were none of the shrill cries of birds and monkeys that we had grown used to, or even the constant chirping of insects. Thinking back, being without the constant cacophony that had plagued us every step of the journey evoked a profound feeling of wrongness. What had caused the jungle to fall silent? Could it sense the Pit just as we had? Worse, had gazing into its depths caused the animals to become overtaken with that feeling our more advanced brains had shaken off? Even now, as night has fallen, the sounds of the jungle are quieter, as though whatever usually makes them is keeping its distance. At least it should be easier to fall asleep. Even Redge is silent tonight.

23 December 1923:

Yet again I awoke to rain. This time it was pounding against the thatch of the hut we had taken shelter in and, in the moments before I opened my eyes, I could imagine that I was back home in England with a light summer shower pattering on my roof. Opening my eyes of course gave truth to the grim reality. The heat of that summer day was still there, but instead of the white walls of my house I saw the dimly lit wood and mud of our borrowed abode. There was a tinge of wood smoke in the air too: someone had lit a fire and was hopefully cooking breakfast.

There's something about sleeping on the ground that makes the aches of the previous day all the more painful, and it was only through supreme effort that I pulled myself to my feet. As I rubbed my sore joints, I saw that my companions were already awake, standing around a furiously smoking fire that was slowly filling the high roof of the hut with a white fog. Martin was poking the fire and muttering glumly to himself; he informed me that, in the night, water had seeped into our fire lighting equipment and soaked it through. As a result, he was struggling to generate enough heat to properly keep the damp logs alight, and the prospect of cooking anything for a hearty breakfast was still hours off at best. Oscar had been sent out to try and find any dry material that could be used to sustain the fire better, although with the rain relentlessly pounding down outside, we knew the chances of that were slim. As Isaacs and Redge were working their way through our packs to see what else the water had gotten into, and the air was starting to become so thick with smoke that I fought back a cough with each breath, I decided I would join Oscar in searching for dry firewood outside. The rain fell in great sheets with far more ferocity than I had ever seen back home in England, and it pummelled like fists against the fabric of my greatcoat.. For a second I debated retreating back inside, but the thick plume of smoke that had followed me out quickly dissuaded me. Hunching under my coat, I stalked out into the downpour and made my way towards the edge of the clearing. I passed other abandoned huts and noticed that some were in states of disrepair. Some of the walls had collapsed inwards and their roofs sagged, allowing dark pools of water to gather in old fire pits and seep out of tilting door frames.

Evidently, in our excitement at discovering this place and its ruins— and our later captivation by the void of the pit— we had failed to notice quite how abandoned this place was. My stomach gave an involuntary twist of vertigo as my mind strayed back to that precipice we had found ourselves on and I staggered, grabbing at the frame of the nearest hut as I did so. The wood cracked as my hand gripped it and it was all I could do to stop myself being trapped under the mass of wet sticks and vegetation that came tumbling down. I lay on the sodden ground, the rain beating relentlessly into my face as I stared up into the grey, cloudy sky. Or was I looking down? For a second, just one brief second, I felt as though I was falling into that grey, endless expanse, and my stomach flipped again— but this time I felt a sense of freedom whispering at the back of my mind. Time did not exist here, and I could fall and fall forever in true freedom.

The next second I felt the coldness of water seeping through the back of my greatcoat and the sky rushed away from me again. I was still on the ground, with sticks and sharp rocks digging into me. I scrabbled at the ground and hauled myself to my feet. The feeling of freedom in an endless expanse was fading as quickly as it had arrived as I stood and tried to pry my now-soaked undershirt away from my back. The feeling didn't quite disappear though. It lurked at the back of my mind, and in a move that I cannot fully say was of my own doing, my head turned to look beyond the now collapsed wall of the hut. The Pit sat there. The feeling pulsed, as though trying to lead me. I took a step towards it. I shook my head, closing my eyes and trying to block out that same desire we had all felt the night before.

Come, it said with something that wasn't quite words, jump, be free. I shook my head and dug my thumbs hard into my palms, feeling the burst of pain blossom in my mind. And then it was gone.

The Pit still sat there, a dark blemish on the skin of the world, and its call still rang in the back of my mind– but I no longer felt its pull with any strength. I was breathing hard, as though I had just run a marathon, and there was sweat running down my face.

I knew then, as I know writing these words, that I should have run. But I couldn't. Whatever it was doing to us, and for all the Pit and this place scared me, I could not find it within myself to force my legs to run. Instead, I resumed my walk towards the edge of the clearing, trying to keep the hungry maw of the Pit from my sight until it was obscured by the trees.

I found Oscar as I was returning to camp, my arms weighed down with wood that had escaped the worst of the downpour still beating its way through the trees. He was standing on a rise at the edge of the clearing, his own arms held out in front of him and the logs lying in a pile at his feet. He had evidently been standing there for some time, as the water had begun to pool around him, and his hair and clothes were completely soaked through. I didn't need to see his face to know where his eyes were fixed. Thankfully, his body obscured that damnable Pit from my own vision.

He started as my hand touched his shoulder; he stared around wildly, as though he had been suddenly woken from a deep sleep. He seemed, for the first time, to notice that his arms were empty, and he scrabbled around trying quickly to pick up the wood. When his eyes flickered to me, I saw something in them that I can only describe as the starkest terror. Without saying a word, he gathered what wood he could and made off towards our hut before I could say anything. I followed after him, averting my eyes from the Pit as I felt them straining in their sockets to move towards it. It was only when I had shut the door of our hut behind me that I felt its presence diminish again, although it never quite vanished.

Oscar was there too, piling his remaining wood onto the still-smoking embers, that look of terror still clear in his eyes as they darted around the room. My other companions didn't seem to have noticed and were in deep conversation as they leant over rolls of papers that had been spread over the floor and contained the beginnings of diagrams sketched in rough black pencil. As I put my wood down and started to make my way over to Oscar, they beckoned us both over. I wanted desperately to talk to him, to ask what he experienced at the Pit and whether he was able to shake it off as I had– but that would have to wait.

I could hear the excitement in Isaacs' voice as I squatted in the dust next to them all. Gone was the quietness of the previous night. Isaacs' enthusiasm to explore and catalogue the ancient ruins surrounding the village had returned with a zeal. It was as though all memory of last night, as we'd stood at the precipice of the Pit, had been wiped from his mind. The only reminder that it existed at all was the scribbled-in circle at the very centre of the rough map he was drawing. He was gesticulating with his hands, excitedly telling Martin what the positions of a certain cluster of ruined walls and arches might mean as the other man looked silently on, never quite meeting his eyes. Isaacs' plan was for the four of us to take a quarter of the map he was drawing, catalogue whatever we found there, and report back to him in the hut where he would put our findings together into one coherent picture. It was hard not to get caught up in his infectious excitement, and soon I had almost forgotten the unexplainable, malevolent presence that lurked mere tens of metres from our shelter.

Surveying the ruins took most of the day. Thankfully the rain had mostly abated, and we were able to head out of our shelter without that particular aspect of nature bothering us. The mosquitoes and humidity became our new enemies though; they swarmed in dark clouds over pools of still water and around our heads where our sweat ran in rivers, unable to evaporate. Each breath felt like it was being taken underwater as the warm, wet air filled our lungs and I began to wish for the rain to return, if only to wash our skin clear of those whining invaders. Still, we separated and began to go about our assigned tasks, and I was soon absorbed in my work, marking down the rough locations of ruined walls and the suggestions of floors that peaked from below smothering green vines swollen with the sudden influx of fresh water. It was getting late, and I was clambering over a crumbling wall to try to get a better angle to sketch the remains of a particularly fascinating fresco on what may have once been a column, when I heard a twig snap heavily behind me.

I froze, my pencil lead splintering over the page as it ground to a halt. My breath caught in my lungs. The only movement was the sweat running from my hairline. We'd had run-ins with jaguars before, normally at night where a lit torch or our sheer numbers had been enough to dissuade them, but I had never been caught off guard by myself. Another twig snapped. It was closer this time. Slowly, I changed my grip on my pencil so I held it like one would hold a dagger. I knew it would be no match against claws and teeth, but it made me feel safer. I would have to be quick to catch it off guard, and hopefully get a strike in before I was taken down. My entire body tensed, and then I whirled, bringing my pencil up in a strike. I was met by a sudden cry and a hand grabbing at my wrist trying to stop my swing.

Oscar was before me, shock flashing through his dark eyes as he stumbled backwards. My heart was hammering in my chest, and I lowered my pencil while cursing him for creeping up on me like that. I sat on the wall and asked him what he was doing here in my quarter. His expression was clouded with the same terror I had seen before, and, again, his eyes darted around as though he was concerned we would be overheard. He said he wanted to talk about the Pit. I asked him if it had affected him as it had me.

He nodded slowly and said in a trembling voice, 'Like a void filling you up, swallowing you, crushing you, pulling you in. There's no power that can fight it. Do you see how it draws in the very world?' His voice trailed off and I opened my mouth to try and tell him that these effects could be fought off, resisted, but he suddenly flinched as though he'd been struck, and his eyes stared widely at me. Were they darker than when I'd seen him earlier? Certainly, in the light it looked as though his pupils had grown to swallow his irises in deep pools of black. Before I could get a closer look, he was gone, sprinting through the undergrowth, uncaring of the thorns and vines that tore at his clothes. Only his panicked voice floated back to me on the wind.

'It will consume us all.'

I sat there a long while before returning to camp. The others were there, including Oscar, although he wouldn't meet my eyes, and avoided conversation with me. He was silent and sat huddled under his thin blanket, far from the fire, for most of the night. Martin brought him a bowl of stew and sat with him for a while but, as far as I could tell, neither said a word to each other. This was vastly out of the ordinary for Oscar, and I was severely worried for the man. I could not bring my concerns to Isaacs however, as he was buoyed by the excitement of the map we had constructed from our surveys. He led us in a toast to the largest ancient settlement found to date, to our names in the history books, and fame and fortune upon our return to England. If he noticed that only myself and Redge joined him for this toast, he gave no sign. After that I gave my excuses and stepped out under the pretence of a smoke before bed.

Oscar's words rang back to me as I skirted the Pit at a distance.

'It draws in the very world... it will consume us all.'

Now as I write this while standing on that rise, as I did

with Oscar this morning, I try not to see the way the huts slump and the trees bend as though blown by a strong unseen wind, all leaning towards that dark hole in the ground. Even the ground subtly slopes down to its maw.

I shiver in the warm air and again think about running, but in the jungle without proper provisions, I would be dead before sunrise. At least here I can create the illusion of safety behind four walls and my thin bedroll. I think I would welcome Redge's whispered words of faith tonight, if only to quell my own thundering mind and the odd silence of this place.

24 December 1923:

Oscar is gone. Isaacs woke me as dawn was breaking across our camp. He was frantic. He told me he'd woken to find Oscar's bedroll empty and had assumed he'd stepped outside, but that there was no sign of him. Quickly, I woke the others; Redge grumbled and cursed until he realised what had happened. Martin just nodded silently as I told him, and I thought I saw his eyes flicker towards the door for a second before refocusing to never quite look me in the eye.

We searched all the buildings in the village, calling Oscar's name the whole time. Isaacs and Redge searched the treeline until the sun was high in the sky, but found nothing. There weren't even any animal tracks that could have indicated an attack by a predator. In fact, I don't think I've seen a single animal for the past two days. I've certainly heard none.

Ultimately, it was Isaacs who found the final trace of Oscar. His shouting brought us all running and we found him kneeling in the wet dirt a little ways from our shelter, peering closely at something on the ground. It was a boot print, matching the tread of those worn by Oscar. There was another print ahead of it, and another, tracks leading away from the structure and through the abandoned village. They were certainly fresh, as the water from the previous day's downpours had not flooded them and we followed them as best we could. They meandered seemingly at random through the crumbling buildings; sometimes we lost them where they looked as though they had stumbled through a half-broken wall or thick mats of plant life. So caught up were we in following our companions' steps, that we didn't realise where we were until they ended abruptly.

It wasn't unexpected, I don't think. There was something within me whispering that this was where we would end up, but I'd pushed it down, thinking it only a symptom of the previous few days. The Pit lay before us. We were mere steps from its edge, and I could clearly see the deep imprint where Oscar's boot had found its edge and he had thrown himself over. Redge told us later that the deepness of the imprint suggested he had put force into his last step. I still don't know whether hearing he most likely jumped is better or worse than imagining Oscar finding himself on the edge of that void and simply stumbling into its depths.

As soon as I realised what lay before us I grabbed Redge and Isaacs and pulled them back, sending them sprawling in the dirt with cries of protest. I then lunged for Martin as he took a single step forward. My hands found his shoulders, and for a few seconds it was as though I was trying to move a boulder. Then his body softened, and I was able to drag him away. All through this he didn't say a word or turn his head from the pit.

We all made our way back to the shelter and sat in silence for a long while. The silence wasn't broken until hours, or maybe just minutes, had passed. It was Martin who broke it. Quiet Martin, whom I am sure I had not heard speak at all until this moment.

'We need to go after him.'

I looked at him in shock and immediately began to protest. We'd all felt that Pit's pull the moment we had arrived here, and we'd nearly all succumbed in that very moment. I told them all how I had felt something drawing me to the Pit every time I set eyes on it. It was evil in some sense that I was sure we could all feel, but couldn't put into words. Redge even backed me up, saying he had avoided going near the thing since our encounter on the first night. He said he'd trusted in God to deliver him from the feelings that had been scratching at the back of his mind from the moment he'd first set foot here.

We looked from Isaacs to Martin, and I saw that Martin was staring directly into Isaacs' eyes. They sat like that for a minute, Isaacs' blue eyes meeting Martin's, the latter looking completely black in the shadows cast across the room. As I had last night, I found myself shivering despite the heat; I looked at Redge, who reached out and gently shook Isaacs shoulder.

Slowly, his eyes never leaving Martin's, Isaacs nodded.

'Yes,' he said softly, 'we must follow him.'

Both myself and Redge began our protests again, but Isaacs cut us off by leaping to his feet and walking to his pack, where he began to collect up one of the long coils of rope we carried for emergencies. Martin rose too and began unpacking his own length of rope.

'I'll come too,' he said, 'you may need some help.' If Isaacs heard him, he gave no indication. His eyes were staring straight ahead, as though at some unseen horizon.

They made their way to the door of our shelter, and myself and Redge made one last attempt to convince them that we needed to leave, that Oscar was lost. For the first time, as I stood before him, I saw anger in Isaacs' expression. His eyes glared deep into mine with an intensity I had not seen before, and I felt something in the corners of my mind shift, telling me to stand aside and let them push past to their doom. I pushed it down and remained motionless in the doorway.

'You can't go,' I told him, trying to keep my voice level as he pressed closer. Isaacs told me to move. His voice was level and monotone but contained an undercurrent of threat that again almost compelled me to stand aside. I swallowed hard and stood firm. He said it again, this time shouting– and then he lunged towards me, his hands impacting my chest. I wasn't prepared for the strength he threw into the push; I stumbled backwards as my legs gave way and sent me sprawling.

I could only stare up at Isaacs as he and Martin left our hut and began to walk towards where the Pit lay waiting behind ruined buildings. Neither of them looked at me as they passed. Their eyes were fixed straight ahead, trance-like, with an intensity that caused the suppressed awareness of the Pit lurking at the back of my mind to twist and swell with what felt like excitement. I felt sick; I knew, deep down, that there was nothing we could do to force them from their paths. They belonged to the Pit now, I was sure. They had fallen to its pull, just as Oscar had. As these thoughts filled my mind, the presence swelled again, and I had to fight the familiar feeling of vertigo that washed over me. I rolled onto my front, retching but bringing up nothing from my empty stomach. The world whirled around me, and I struggled to focus on a point to bring me back to some semblance of reality. The ground felt as though it were tilting, sloping ever downwards towards that ever-waiting Pit, and I was convinced my body was about to start sliding uncontrollably towards it. I tried to scream, but my very breath felt as though it had been stolen from me.

Then there was a rough hand grabbing my shoulder, and I was being hauled to my feet. My head slowly stopped spinning as Redge's concerned face swam into focus in front of me. One hand was still gripping me, the other holding the roughly carved wooden cross still attached to the leather thong that looped around his neck. I thanked him and he nodded gravely. There was little for us to say. We had never truly gotten on throughout our expedition, but we could both recognise the extreme danger we found ourselves in.

We found Isaacs and Martin at the mouth of the Pit, working quickly to attach their ropes to the closest huts. They didn't seem to notice our approach, although our footsteps sounded deafening against the silence that constantly filled our surroundings. It was hard to simply stop ourselves at the outer layer of huts and watch our companions prepare to descend. Perhaps due to the proximity of the Pit's pull, or maybe even a desire to make one final attempt to save my companions, my feet had already taken two steps beyond the final wall and down the slope to the waiting precipice before Redge's arm shot out and caught me. I could see the strain on his face as he pulled me back into the shadow of a half-collapsed hut. I was feeling the pull of the Pit now that it was in view, and my legs were not easily persuaded to move in any direction other than towards it.

Redge was muttering something. It was a low rhythmic chant under his breath and one of his hands was again clasped at the cross. It took me a minute to recognise The Lord's Prayer, so long had it been since I had purposefully engaged in any form of religion. Yet, as I concentrated on those words and their flowing rhythm, I found the power the Pit held over me being forced out, like the sin from the body of a confessing man. I shall admit I have no aptitude for religious metaphor, but I believe in that moment, as I began to intone the words with such conviction and faith in my own mind, I felt its evil presence purged from my body and I felt true hope for the first time in days.

As the repeating words burned in my mind, I found my own faith returning stronger than ever, like a tidal wave, and I was able to look upon the Pit and truly feel nothing. None of its pull, or even of the enticement to gaze deeper into its depths. I had left faith behind on the battlefields of France, believing no caring God could allow such slaughter, but I saw now its true power: as a barrier to those devilish things that would lure and trick us into the damnation of their depths. What did God care for the squabbles of humanity when the world played host to this very aspect of Satan made manifest? An aspect our companions were in the process of being swallowed by?

They were descending now, their bodies already up to their waists below the rim. They held onto the ropes with a white knuckled grip. Their faces were blank, their eyes black pools staring blindly ahead, and I knew there was nothing that we could do to save them. Still, I broke free of Redge's arm and stepped once more into the open, still feverishly reciting The Lord's Prayer in my head. I had to try something, you see, even if I could not tell them that all they must do is have faith and they will be delivered from this evil. I did not know if they could still comprehend my words, or if they had fallen to the Pit so completely to have left everything human behind. Still, I had to try.

I shouted to Isaacs as they sank lower, hoping, praying that something of my words would make it through. 'Isaacs! You can fight this, this evil. We'll wait one day, and God willing you will return to us.'

He looked at me as I spoke, I'm sure. I tiny almost imperceptible twitch of his head in my direction and those inky black eyes met my own, and then he was gone below the surface. The next moment Redge was bundling me back away from the Pit and towards our hut, still muttering that lifesaving prayer. I don't know whether Isaacs found the strength to fight, or if he even heard my words but I do know that, as I spoke His name, the ever-present sense of the Pit that had settled in my mind seemed to pull away entirely. It was almost enough for me to laugh out loud with relief.

Over the next few hours, we took it in turn reading verses or prayers from Redge's Bible to stave off the presence that seemed to be trying harder than ever to worm its way back into our minds. I found those passages that held an almost song-like rhythm to be most effective, for they filled my mind most completely and we were able to accomplish most basic tasks while in this thrall of religious devotion. I was determined to be true to my word to Isaacs, no matter how slim any chances of his emergence were. We would have to wait a day and then make for the nearest indigenous settlement and hope that we could find our way home from there. I also burned

Isaacs' maps of this place, leaving only one that would take us to safety before it too would be destroyed. There would be no record of this place having ever existed, so that no unfortunate travellers like ourselves could stumble upon it and be enthralled as we all had so nearly been.

The sun had started to sink in the sky, and we had begun to prepare ourselves for bed when we heard a man's voice call from outside. In a second I was on my feet, my mind racing; for a brief moment, I thought it was Isaacs and the others returned to us. But then I heard a woman's voice join the first and realised who had entered our camp.

To Andrew and Amelia, we must have looked quite the sight, like street preachers of years gone by, with Redge chanting aloud prayers to keep at bay the evil of the Pit as I led us through the huts to meet them. Luckily for them, they had entered the village on a side that hid the Pit from their sight, so I doubt they felt its immediate effects. I am sure they thought us quite mad when we emerged in front of them. Amelia's face lit up as she saw us, but her expression soon turned to confusion and concern at Redge's continual chanting as we hurriedly ushered her and Andrew towards our shelter.

Just once, for a second between buildings, we passed within view of the Pit. Andrew and Amelia were asking us questions, but I hardly heard; I was focused on the rhythm in my mind, pushing back at the Pit's presence as it came into our eye-line. For whatever reason, however, the newfound protection of our faith did not extend to Andrew and Amelia. As if on some invisible cue, their heads turned, and their eyes went blank as their feet began to turn towards the Pit. This only happened for a moment, for we pushed them past this gap and they stumbled onwards, letting out long gasping breaths as though the air had been suddenly caught in their lungs. Every now and then, as we neared the shelter, one of them would glance back over their shoulder with a look that could only be described as longing flashing across their face.

Once the door was closed, they began bombarding us with questions again. It seemed as though they had forgotten the Pit's influence for their questions started off simple and innocent. How had we all been, what discoveries had we made here, did we have any trouble catching tortoises? Things took a more serious turn, I think, when they noticed we didn't laugh at the final question. Redge, who had kept up his soft chanting, closed his eyes and spoke louder, cutting through their laughter. I understood why, for in the brief instant their laughter had drowned him out, I had felt the first stomach-flipping pangs of vertigo invade my senses. I held on to his words and the feeling faded, but I saw the glance that was shared between the other two. Their expressions hardened and they began demanding to know where the others were and what had happened here. Eventually, Amelia threw her pack to the ground and shouted at Redge to stop praying for one goddamn minute. I saw a flicker of fear cross Redge's face, but he shook his head and continued, turning to block out the glares he was receiving. I tried to explain to them what had happened. I started with our discovery of the Pit, even showed them a few of my previous journal entries and explained how faith kept the evil at bay. I could tell that, although they didn't know what was happening here, they didn't believe a word I said. Andrew, who knew of my previous dislike of religion stated that my sudden conversion to, as he put it, a rabid believer, meant I must have truly gone mad.

After that there was little more to say, and night was settling in. Before they wrapped themselves in their bedrolls and covered their ears to block out Redge's prayers, I made them promise that no matter what, they would not venture outside during the night. They agreed, although I could tell it was only to keep us happy.

Redge and I are going to sleep too. We are comforted by the idea that tomorrow we will depart this place, never to return.

25 December 1923:

This will be my last log.

It is Christmas day, I think. I do not know how long I have lain here. Pain and exhaustion are close to claiming me, but I must chronicle these last few hours, even though, if you are reading them, you must have fallen to the same fate as myself.

I shouldn't be here. None of us should have ever set foot into these unknown, unexplored spaces of the world. What we've found in here should never have been uncovered and I am sure it will ultimately spell doom for us all. I should be back in England with my wife, my son. I should be watching him play with his toys in the flickering light of the tree, secure in the knowledge that the most potent terrors of the world have been left far behind. Now I understand the meaning of Thomas Gray's phrase, ignorance is bliss.

I can feel it. It's in my head and it whispers such terrible things.

But I must finish this whole sorry tale before I succumb. I have held on this long, after all, even if that strength was merely a ridiculous falsehood meant to ensnare us.

It was the rain that woke us. Not pouring from the sloped roof of our hut in a gushing torrent, as it had on previous nights, but whipping across our faces and soaking through our thin blankets. Redge had awoken before me, and I could hear him softly intoning a prayer as he rummaged about in the darkness to light our remaining candle. Our fire had long since burned down to a gently smouldering ruby glow.

His voice brought an immediate comfort to me, as I had been dreaming of an infinite void of total blackness into which I was watching myself fall and which seemed to grow in enormity around me until I was but a speck against its vast, crushing might. I saw myself disappear as it enveloped me and its presence wrapped around my very being, forcing the air from my lungs and smothering my mouth and nose. I think it left my eyes, for what use are they when there is no light to enter them? But I digress. It enjoys– I have realised as I sit here in the blackness, lit only by that same singular candle– basking in the fear its presence creates, and it is taking everything I have not to give in and let it consume me as it did my companions. Not yet, at least.

I awoke gasping the thick humid air of the jungle into my lungs and, as Redge's words filled my mind and more water droplets flicked across my face, I felt the invading presence fade away once more. I lay there for a minute, catching my breath and concentrating on his words as the candle flared into life. It was as I was pulling myself up on my elbows, that I heard his voice raise in alarm. Though he was shielding the flame from the rain which still lashed at us, I could still see the empty bedrolls in the corner. Cold dread seeped into my heart. The door had been thrown wide open, allowing the wind and rain to blow freely inside.

Andrew and Amelia were gone.

Redge was out of the hut before myself, shouting their names into the night, although we both knew where they had gone. I shrugged on my greatcoat, though it was of little use when the rest of me was already wet through, and bowed my head against the rain as I followed Redge outside. It didn't take me long to find him, for the light of the moon still shone dimly through the clouds. He was standing a little way from the entrance, still shouting their names; he turned to face me as I approached him.

I shot a glance towards the Pit, and he nodded slowly. Again, no words need be said between us. The memories of our fruitless search for Oscar just a day before were worming their way back into our minds, and I joined Redge in whispering a prayer as the presence latched onto these thoughts and tried to slip its way in amongst them. We pushed it back, and, with our heads seemingly clear, we focused on the duty at hand. Even under the light of the moon we tripped and stumbled on our way through ruined huts and along paths that were turning to slippery quagmires.

I expected, as we arrived at the Pit, only footprints in the mud. Had that been the case, we may have found ourselves in happier circumstances than those I am now doomed to find my end in. Instead, we found Andrew and Amelia standing at the precipice of the Pit, gazing into its depths, just as the five of us had upon our arrival in that clearing. They did not look at us as we arrived, doubtless caught in the same trancelike state as the others.

I shouted to them, trusting in Redge to keep our faith strong, though if I caught their attention, they gave no sign. I advanced towards them. In that moment I held no fear of the Pit and felt none of its malign influence on my mind. With Redge at my back intoning the words of the Lord and brandishing his cross, I felt invincible to its beguiling influence.

Doubtless, his voice travelled to them too. I was but mere feet away from pulling them back from the edge when, as one, they fell. It could almost be described as graceful. One moment they stood at the drop, their backs straight and arms rigid by their sides. Then, in perfect synchronisation, their bodies leant forwards and they were gone.

I will say that this loss broke me. I was so close. Had I been quicker, I could have pulled them back and saved them from their fate. Grief swept over me; I fell to my knees, pounding the soft mud with my fists and weeping into the dirt.

Looking back, I see the Pit's sick machinations at work, and I know I could not have saved them. I know too, it was this moment when I sealed the fates of both Redge, and myself.

I wasn't thinking; my mind was a blur of loss and anger. Our entire party, gone in the space of two days. Swallowed by this hole in the ground, a hole that seemed to bleed devilish influence like blood seeping from a deep wound. The aftermath is a blur of emotions, of Redge pulling me back from the edge and brandishing his cross as he prayed for the Devil to be cast out of this land.

When I felt the rope in my hands, I knew what I was doing. If I couldn't rescue my companions, then I would recover their bodies, so they were not damned to whatever hell this place had in store for them.

My feet swung over the precipice, and I saw the rope below me, disappearing into a darkness that somehow seemed so much more complete than that of the night air. The call was stronger here, and I began praying out loud to banish it, lest my strength of will failed and I hauled myself back over the edge to solid ground. When Redge joined me, I saw in his eyes the same determination that I felt. In those moments, as we began our descent, I believed we had won. My rediscovered faith had given me the strength to overcome the Devil residing here; we would descend into its depths untouched, and bring salvation to the bodies of our companions.

After twenty minutes of descent my mouth was dry, and my arms were screaming from the constant exertion. I'd left my canteen next to my bedroll, and silently cursed myself for it between verses of the Lord's Prayer. Each time my voice faltered, I felt the presence loom in my mind and threaten to cast me from the rope into the waiting depths. More than once, those thoughts almost made me turn back, but with the beginning of each new verse I was reminded of the strength of my re-found faith and so I continued, hand over hand, foot over foot, deeper and deeper into the waiting earth.

Redge seemed to be having a harder time than me, his breathing becoming laboured, his voice catching in his throat. He had to stop frequently to rest. I wanted nothing more to continue deeper, to stop at nothing until we found our companions, but I forced myself to wait and do nothing save gaze up at the pinprick of light above us, all that remained of the surface world and the moonlit sky. How deep we were I had no idea. Certainly we were deeper than the fifty-foot length of each rope, but the strangeness of that fact did not concern me at the time. Perhaps it should have.

After another ten minutes I realised Redge had stopped again. He was babbling something this time, his head pressed against the thick rope and his eyes shut tight. I swung myself towards him, as close as I could, and asked if he was alright. He fell silent, and looked at me with an expression of such terror and that it was all I could do not to fall from my rope in shock. His next words etched themselves into my mind and I am certain they will remain there until I cease to be.

'No, no, no, we were lied to, we must get out. It knows, it knows.' He hissed these words as a child may tell a secret they do not want overheard, and I asked him what he was talking about. 'It knows we're here, right where it wants us. It tricked us, do you see? I can hear it, in my head, it whispers, oh God it whispers. And the things it says. It was old when our God was young. It was here, the darkness. And it consumed, it consumed then starved then consumed again. Countless aeons beneath the earth, and now it will consume again.' Redge's eyes were rolling back in his head at this point, and his hand scrabbled at something inside his jacket. Tears rolled from the corners of his eyes, but he didn't seem to notice as he softly sobbed the final words he would ever say to me. 'It let us pray, encouraged it. It drew back until we thought we were safe and now, it has us all the same.' With that, as the realisation of his words swept through me, Redge pulled his knife from his jacket and began to saw feverishly through the rope. With a final choking sob, his rope snapped, and he plunged down to be swallowed by the Pit.

I panicked. I felt the presence press in and sweep aside my desperate prayers for salvation with an ease that told me they had never affected it in the first place. It had merely wanted us to think so. I tried to pull myself back up the rope, up towards that tiny point of sky, but my hands were slick with sweat from my panic and my grip failed, sending me plunging after Redge.

The fall felt timeless. It could have been as long as a million years or as short as a handful of seconds, but I was surrounded on all sides by darkness. It clustered around me in a suffocating mass, on and on, until I felt sure I would fall forever. The feeling of ground beneath me again was sudden and brutal. My legs impacted first. I felt something snap, sending a lance of pain through me as my body slammed into the ground. I lay there for a long time before I felt able to move again. There was something digging into my side, and I felt around with my aching arm until I pulled the thing out and held it before my face. There was no light in this place, so I had to rely on my hands to feel and work out what it was. Its surface was soft and waxy and, from the way it tapered at one end, I realised it was Redge's candle. It had been with him when he had fallen so how it had ended up under me, I had no idea. I called out his name, but the darkness swallowed it, and I heard no reply. Still, I could at least try and see where I was. I fished around in my coat pockets and found the box of matches I have always kept in there. With some difficulty, trying not to move my shattered leg, I lit the candle.

I was lying in a tiny earthen tunnel that closed in on me from all sides. Where the hole to the mouth of the Pit should have been there was only a low roof and, although I tried to shine the light of the candle further down the tunnel, I saw only darkness. I have never considered myself claustrophobic, but in that instant, it was as though the entire weight of the world was pressing down on me and I screamed, thrashing my arms around and gouging clumps of cold, dry earth from the tunnel wall.

I don't know when I started writing this down, or why I had tucked my journal and pencil into my jacket pocket as I had left the hut. Did the Pit know, even then, how this all would end? Does it get some pleasure from watching me scribble away my final moments in madness and despair? Perhaps I went mad the moment I watched Isaacs and Martin descend into these awful depths. It certainly feels that way now.

I can feel it. It's in my head and it whispers such terrible things. Of a world willingly drawn into a void from which there can be no escape. A void which grows silently in the corners of civilisation, consuming all before they even know the danger they are in.

This is what it wanted. It tricked us, myself and Redge, I see it now. It knew we were strong-willed enough together to defy its call directly, so it made us think we had beat it. It came forth, then withdrew with each useless expression of faith until we were sure we could withstand its influence. Then, masquerading as the assurance of that faith, it drew us into the earth regardless. It is no Devil, no thing that can be cast out through prayer or belief. It is something more. Unknowable, malevolent. It will feast on us before the end.

The candle is burning low. There's not long left, and I know when only darkness remains and my mind is filled with Its twisting call, It will consume me, as It has my fellows, and as It will consume us all.

Breath Upon A Candle Flame

J. Morfa

For N. I think you'd have liked this one.

"You have the grimoire, my child?" Father Heather's harsh voice. Low. Echoing off the walls of the confessional. Husk of sixty five year's tobacco. Eerie. Evil. Malicious.
Did not speak at first. Only stared at the tome in my lap. Felt heavy.
"I have it," I said at length. Whispering. Quiet.
Grating of the confessional divide being moved aside. Scream of rust scraping against wood. Withered, calloused claw. Crept through. Tapped four times upon the shelf. Demanding. Wanting.
"Pass it here, my child. Pass it here, Aurelius," said the claw.
No reluctance on my part. An unearthly sound as the

book slipped across the hardwood shelf. Through the grate. Into oblivion.

I could not see his eyes. They must have glistened in the flame of the candelabra on the wall beside his head. He was smiling. I could tell by his voice. The glee. The pointed edge of a cackle. Years searching. Years sending fools such as myself on foolish quests for the black grimoire known as Scientia Universalis. The key to Heaven. Now Father Heather finally held his heart's desire.

"My child, it is beautiful!"

A choke. The guttering of a candle when it has run out of wick or wax. When the flame suffocates. When it breathes its last.

I knew he would die. Knew before then. Knew as far back as the day I first sought him out. If his death had not been by the book I would have pierced his heart with my stiletto. For his cruelty. For his evil. For all the grief he had brought into the world. For every loathsome deed. Father Heather had to die. Father Heather deserved it.

He'd ignored the warnings that Scientia Universalis was cursed. Ignored that it brought death upon all those who opened it. Ignored the legend which claimed only the worthy, only those without sin, or to speak more wisely, nobody at all, could open the grimoire. Could live to speak of the knowledge within.

Father Heather had once scoffed at his mentor, Abbot Aquinas, when he was still a novice at Carnforth Abbey.

"How do they know?"

"I would assume, perhaps, maybe, because their deaths were witnessed by their companions," Abbot Aquinas said. "Perhaps those companions were not so foolish as to think themselves worthy of opening the book. The legend does state it is an act of folly."

"It is not folly for a man who is without sin. One who is pure," Heather huffed.

"Which of us is without sin? Which of us was not born of woman?"

Heather sauntered to the heart of the cloister where the pair strolled. He plucked an apple from the tree. Weighed it in his hand. Pondered on the consequences of the second story, that which tells how each of us came to be tainted by original sin. Tainted because the Devil tempted Eve with knowledge which was forbidden. Tainted because God cursed humankind for their wickedness.

"I will find the grimoire," Heather said. "I will open it. I will know the knowledge it contains. I will not die."

"My son," Abbot Aquinas said, watching as Heather tossed the apple away. "There are none who have set eyes on the tome for thirteen hundred years. Not since the unenlightened age which followed the Romans. Not since before Saint Augustus claimed these islands for God."

"If that is so, then perhaps the curse is no more than a myth, Father Abbot. Perhaps it is only a yarn intended to keep people from seeking the book. Perhaps the curse is a fairy story."

"Or perhaps the grimoire itself is the fairy story?"

Fairy story?

The supposed fairy story lay at the feet of Father Heather. Father Hakeswill Heather. Horrid, hateful, tiny old man, whose only hairs were five independent white wires protruding from his chin- Thick splinters of wood. Slumped. Dead in his confessional coffin. Eyes open. Shocked by the death spectre which had materialised before him. Ringed claw resting on his knee, pointing towards me. Accusatory.

"You, Aurelius," his immortal shade spoke from beyond the grave. "You caused my death. You, Godless sinner, have taken my life!"

Yes. I did. I killed you, Father Heather. I allowed you to take the book from me. I knew you would die when you opened it. Had you not quested your whole life for that book? The book whose legend foreshadows death? Had you not sent so many others to die in your place? Does The Bible not mention an eye for an eye, a life for a life?

Did you not open the book willingly? Did you not suspect when you opened it you might die like all the rest? Was there never a doubt in your mind about your worthiness?

No. There was not.

"I am a man of God," Heather declared. "I am without sin. How can a man of God be with sin?"

"Many a holy brother or holy sister has been led into dark temptation," Abbot Aquinas would have answered. Father Heather did not listen. Father Heather would not listen.

I wondered. What was his sin?

Lust.

Lust for the grimoire. Lust for Scientia Universalis.

Egotism too. The mistaken belief that he alone was worthy of opening the book. He alone worthy of knowing what was within. The belief that he was a man without sin. Also arrogance. Arrogant thoughts that he deserved to hold the book in his hands. He deserved the knowledge within. Also indifference, the indifference he showed in sending so many unfortunate confessors off in pursuit of the book. Indifference towards the deaths he had a hand in.

His crime was murder. Does the bible not say: thou shalt not kill? Is murder not a mortal sin?

Yes, Father Heather. I did kill you. I murdered you. But you murdered so many more than I. Countless unknowns to my one. Countless against you. I only sent you to your rightful doom.

I blew out the lamp on the wall. The flame died. Left only a smouldering firefly at the end of the wick. A childhood rhyme came to me.

Lay your breath upon a candle flame,
Softly, sweetly, speak my name.
With one swift kiss sing death's refrain,
To cast me from this mortal plain.

Apt. I had placed my breath upon Father Heather's already cooling flame. I had sung death's refrain. Cast him from this mortal plain. Surrendered unto him the book which would kill him. All men who open the Scientia Universalis must die according to the legend.

I picked up the book from the floor. Held it under my arm. Stood in the doorway of the confessional. Staring into the void from where Father Heather's soul accurately accused me of his murder. I closed the door. Felt nothing within me. No care. No guilt. No remorse. Soul as empty as the confessional void which caressed Father Heather's corpse.

"Aurelius? Is it done?"

The voice came from a man bathed in the rainbow light of the church's rose window. Angelic. A spectral six foot. Carrying himself with supremest confidence. Supremest certainty. Staring at a marble memorial plaque on the wall. Carved with bones. Skeletons. Visions of the underworld. Black hair hung loose about his shoulders. A sadness I had never seen before swum in his eyes. A burdensome thought carried on his back. From the way he was staring at the memorial I guessed it was somebody gone from this world. An infatuation. A recent passing. Not an unexpected one, however.

"Eldrick. I did not expect you here, Brother."

"I did not expect to be here." He moved from the memorial. Strode down the central aisle. Nodded at me. Gave no other sign of affection.

"You are okay, Aurelius?"

"I shall be."

"May I?"

Eldrick opened the door of the confessional. With a sulphur match he re-lit the lamp. Summoned the body of Father Heather, along with the rotten-egg stench of the underworld, back from the void. He knelt down beside the body. Felt the wrist for a pulse. Closed the accusatory eyes.

"Requiescat in pace," he said, moving away. "Died of

cardiac arrest. The book is the Scientia, I assume?"

I did not need to check, but I held it out in front of me nonetheless. Black leather cover. Rich engraving of serpents. Dragons. Questing beasts. Golden clasp still unlatched. As far as anybody needed to be concerned it was Scientia Universalis.

When I answered Eldrick nodded. Understanding. Not saying a word. He blew out the lamp again. Returned Father Heather to the void.

I repeated the rhyme.

"You doubt yourself," Eldrick said, "doubt you did right in giving the old man his heart's desire."

"Would you have given him the book?"

"No," Eldrick said. "But then I would not have gone searching for it, even if he had asked me."

"You once said that even the idea of the book was poppycock, as I recall."

"I did. Perhaps I was much mistaken, Brother."

Poppycock? That was three years ago. A seedy Abermaw shipbuilder's tavern. Reeking to high heaven of sea salt. Sedition. Would hardly have known it was a tavern. Suppose that is what the Jacobites wanted. From the outside it looked like a peasant cottage. Whitewashed. Windows which bowed outwards. Chimney on the verge of tumbling. Whole building on the verge of crumbling. It was at the top of a set of rickety stone steps which had long brought unexpected widowhood to the wives of Abermaw's dockyard drunkards.

"The cause is not dead," Eldrick said of the Jacobites. Whether we were in Abermaw to help or hinder the cause he would not say. All he said was he needed a second. Somebody to help him observe. Listen.

"Down with the rump," an old man hissed at us.

"God save King Charles!" Eldrick said, raising his pewter tankard. The old man grinned. Replied in kind. Bowed. Left us to our drinks for a while. Without that answer he would have killed us.

We returned to the tavern for three nights following.

Acting the part of Jacobite sympathisers. Came to know the people there. Started to like them. Not as vile, villainous as government propaganda had us believe. The old man who approached us on the first day, Victor, was a darling. Storyteller of the first rate. Victor's stories kept us spellbound during all three of our visits.

Final night, when Victor joined us, he began to tell how he, with his son John, had made to join up with the Scots army during the Forty Five. Victor advanced a hair-raising yarn of encounters with the English Army on the road. Told us how the Jacobite army had already turned back for Scotland by the time they reached Manchester.

"We followed, of course," he said. "Got as far as Ravenglas. There's this church to the north of the village. All surrounded by untended graves. Lonely. Ever so lonely. Cold. Godless. I warned young John we should not tarry. Nay, Father, he said to me. I must make confession for I saw a right fine lady in the last village. Got ever so lusty I did. He was a good Catholic boy, young John. Honest. True. But always an eye for the ladies. That was his failing. He had such faith. Whenever he sinned it was a mighty weight upon him. I told him to wait for the next church. Till we reached the next parish. He insisted on taking his confession at that godforsaken place."

Victor began to speak all reproachful. All bitter. Fingers curled so angrily about his tankard they began to crush it.

"The priest there. Father Heather. Father Hakeswill Heather. A more hateful man I never met. Don't know if it was the isolation up there or something else, but he seemed crazed. There was a mania in his eyes. A madness. There was an archdeacon in Paris some centuries ago. Frollo. They say he had the same madness in his eyes. Aye. Same thing. Lust. A burning, ungodly desire."

"We well know the legend of Claude Frollo," I said. "Had the fancy for a young maiden as I recall. Esme was it? This priest had lust for a maiden?"

"Nay. Not a maiden. Not even a beast bad as it would

have been. No. He had the lust for knowledge. For a book!"

Eldrick slammed his tankard down. A grin. A stare of surprise.

"Was it a naughty book?"

"With naughty engravings?"

"You mock, boys. Father Heather sore wanted that book. He wanted that book as a boy hankers after the pretty village girl who is beyond his league. Desired it. Wanted it because it is reputed special. Rare. Rare as they come. A legendary tome." Eldrick rolled his eyes.

"Yes. The thing about legendary tomes… Even if they ever did exist they don't anymore. After about five or six hundred years most books get destroyed by flood or fire. Or a war comes along to burn down the library, or a King Henry to dissolve the monastery. This Heather was lusting after a fantasy if you ask me."

"He may have been. It is said this book he lusts after hasn't been seen since before the time of the Saxons. It is known as Scientia Universalis."

Eldrick burst out laughing. He was silenced with a serious look. Was interested by what the old man had to say. What was Scientia Universalis? Why was it so special? Why did this priest, this Father Hakeswill Heather, lust after the book?

"I am sorry, Brother, but have you heard of Scientia Universalis? It is poppycock. Nonsense of the first rate. There's more chance of the Duke of Cumberland volunteering to be turned into sausage meat than there is of the Scientia existing."

"Yes, but what is it?"

"A grimoire. Book of knowledge. Cursed to the touch. Said to describe the world which lies beyond our comprehension. The one in the corners of our eyes. It talks of the creatures which can be found there. Hideous half forms. Dogs. Black shades. Monsters. Demons which must never be unleashed on the living."

"The old priest called it the key to Heaven."

"Do you know how it got the nickname, my darling Mr Victor? According to legend it will bring instantaneous death to all who open it. Only he without sin may read it. In other words, nobody."

Victor was silent. When he continued to speak he stared into the half empty, crushed tankard in his hands.

"May I continue my story? As I was saying. Young John felt the need to confess. Since this priest was the only man there, it fell to him to hear the boy.

"I will absolve you of your sin, child, said Father Heather to Young John. But before I do so, you must bring me a holy relic. A book. Bring me the key to Heaven. Bring me Scientia Universalis. Take the road less travelled to the priory at Birkenhead. There, seek out Brother Greene. Tell him Father Hakeswill Heather has sent another champion to claim Scientia Universalis. Do not read it, but return it to me when you have it." The old priest would use the exact same words the same day I confessed at Ravenglas, some time after Abermaw.

"John, in search of absolution, said he had no choice but to take on the wicked priest's quest. My immortal soul is more important than the Jacobite cause, Father, he said to me before he rode south. I could not argue, for he was right. Nothing is more important than our immortal souls.

"When he did not return I wrote to Brother Greene at Birkenhead, seeking news. A different priest, the prior, wrote back. Four more penitents had come his way since my John. All sent by Father Heather. All discovered dead on the Mersey shore at Eastham. Including my John."

"The grimoire killed them?"

"That is what the prior at Birkenhead would have had me believe."

"Tosh. Nonsense. I'm not doubting they were killed, I grieve with you for your loss, my friend, but the grimoire is a fairy story. Those deaths were more likely the result of an accident or some human malice, rather than a literary or supernatural death."

"As I said. It is what the prior would have had me

believe. Here, however, is a definitive truth, which I also learned from the prior. Father Heather, for I do not know how many years, has been sending confessors to Birkenhead Priory to claim the book for his own glory. Almost all, perhaps all, have been found washed up on the shore. They die as a consequence of Heather's lust for the book. His lust for the knowledge it contains. He is responsible for their deaths. Father Heather is a murderer."

It was not my immediate intent to ride for Ravenglas, see the priest for myself, but Victor's story played on my mind. I was not concerned for Scientia Universalis or whatever was written within. What need had I for a book describing things which did not exist? The idea of a book which could kill intrigued me, but Eldrick had this irritating habit of always being correct. They would feed Cumberland into sausage skin before any cursed grimoire was found. It was what Victor had said regarding murder which concerned me. How the priest's lust for knowledge was driving souls towards a tragic ending. It warranted investigation. Warranted resolution. A conclusion. My conscience would not permit acts so terrible to go unchecked.

"I will ride for Ravenglas," I said to Eldrick the last time we were together. We were sheltering in the portico of St Paul's Cathedral one morning in early spring. Old tuppeny prostitute, as per usual, plying her sinful wares on the steps. Calling for the men folk to come feed her little birds. Few takers. Rain coming down solid. Folk shivering in their sodden cloaks. Eldrick was one of the few without a cloak and still as dry as old sawdust.

"I have told you, Aurelius. Scientia Universalis does not exist. What do you want a cursed grimoire for?"

"It is not the grimoire I want, but justice. Resolution. Truth. I wish to know more of this Father Heather. More about the confessors he has sent to die. I seek a rational explanation for what I have been told. I seek justice. You can understand that, can you not, Eldrick?"

"To seek a rational explanation is a noble thing. But this... I do not understand. You have no connection with the dead or with the country. It is not a matter of importance. He is a conspiratorial old priest who will be dead in a few years. He may be dead already. What will a rational explanation achieve?"

"It will help put Victor's mind at ease, to know how his son died. To know what he died for."

"For the folly of an evil man. No more explanation is needed." Eldrick sounded cruel. I did not like him when he spoke in such a way. "Justice? I can understand justice, Brother, but it is not our justice to serve. It is a justice which must be left for others."

My mind was already made up. I begged Eldrick to accompany me. He refused.

"This is not a quest you need to undertake. There are more important matters to be dealt with. A lusty priest in the back-end of the North can wait, if he must be handled at all."

"I cannot allow it to wait. How many more shall die whilst we wait? Would you have the deaths of those men on your conscience? I cannot have them on mine."

Eldrick insisted the matter was folly up until the moment of our goodbye. Think he worried I would die like all the others. There was certainly sorrow in his voice when he bid me farewell. I was determined not to die, however. Was determined whatever had caused the deaths of those who had confessed I would not share the same fate.

Thus, I rode north for Ravenglas – Along the Western road to Bristol, up through Worcestershire, Shropshire, stopping at Chester to make enquiries into Brother Greene. The priory at Birkenhead.

"Awful place up there," they would say. "Marsh country. Boggy. Odd. Blighted land it is. I've not heard of Brother Greene. Speaking of green though, you know the Green Knight is said to have had his chapel up that way somewhere? The one who challenged Sir Gawain?" Aye,

I had known. Sir Gawain's fate was not the pitiful tale I was seeking an answer to, however.

I asked after others who had sought Brother Greene or the priory, but nobody I found in Chester had met anyone. Nobody had heard of Brother Greene.

"If they're coming from Ravenglas, as you say," one man suggested, "They'll be taking the ferry from Liverpool."

Time was pressing. I needed to reach Ravenglas with haste.

Eldrick wrote to say he was riding for Lancaster on another matter. Thought I could meet him on the road, assist him if my own business was resolved quickly enough.

The church at Ravenglas appeared abandoned. Some miles outside the village. In the most desolate country possible. As desolate as I was to find on Wirral. It was exactly as Victor had described. Cold. Godless. Faith buried somewhere in the tumbledown graveyard surrounding the church. Evil here. Tending to the tombs. Watching for the unwary sinner. The building had claws. Limbs. Two dead branches reaching out from the slates of the spire, reaching out for heaven in a futile prayer. The building an unburied corpse in the centre of the graveyard. Wretched. Decaying. Rotting.

I hated it. Despised it. Place was a boil on the body of Christ. Uncomfortable. Unwelcoming. Inhospitable place in an unwelcoming inhospitable backwater. Sort of place where you would expect to find a bandit. A brigand. A rogue. Exactly the kind of person to callously cast unwitting travellers towards misfortune. This was witch country. Devil-demon land. An evil edifice which took great courage to approach. A place for the devil to recite matins.

I go on. I assume you get the picture. Father Hakeswill Heather slithered from his den at the creaking of the church door. Eyes flashed when he saw me. Mouth turning downwards into a grimace. Then he smirked.

Recognised prey. A victim.

Played up to the part.

"Father. I have sinned," I said. "I must confess for the sake of my immortal soul."

"How grave is your sin, my child?"

"Grave. Oh so grave. Ever so grave. Leviticus. Eighteen twenty two."

"Thou shalt not lie with a man as with a woman, for it is an abomination," Father Heather quoted. Almost dancing. Never had such a vile sinner entered his church. I had indeed done the thing of which I'd told him. Though he was an evil man I could not in all good conscience confess to things I had not done. He was still a priest. I could not lie to a priest in such a way. Something in my upbringing stopped me, told me it was not right to do so.

"Did you enjoy it? Did you revel in your sodomy?"

"It was not sodomy. It was more a form of onanism. But yes. I revelled in it. I have dreamed of it with increasing regularity." Again, no lie.

"It is the devil taunting you for your sins. He is making you relive it all. Tempting your soul to sin again."

"I must end it, Father. Please, Father. Can you absolve me of my sin? I go mad with this devil upon my conscience!" Only untruth I told that day.

"It is difficult, but no one is beyond the mercy of The Lord." Then Father Heather said the same words he had said to so many others. It was, I hope, the last time. "I will absolve you of your sin, my child."

Given the quest for Scientia Universalis. The road less travelled to Birkenhead Priory. To Brother Greene.

I might have murdered Father Heather then. He had readily convicted himself of the crimes for which he stood accused. But there was the business of Scientia Universalis to attend to first. Alas. I needed to first discover how the confessors had come to die before justice was served. Before he died.

Ergo. I returned south.

Liverpool in those days was not the great metropolis it has today become. Was making strides in that direction though. Strangers, sailors, salt baked seamen, all frequented city taverns in significant numbers. Thus, it seemed folly to ask after those who sought Brother Greene. This was a port where strangers, visitors, were becoming all too common. Few would recall any specific individual. Too many people passed through here now. After a while they all looked the same. Asking the locals about strangers, asking strangers about other strangers, would yield little.

Chance found me. Perhaps not chance, given what I later discovered. Perhaps fate?

First morning in the town. Observing Birkenhead Priory from the quayside. An aged, gnarled man, cutpurse no doubt, approached me. Thin. Colour grey. Muddy grey. Colour the waters of the river. If he stood perfectly still he would have resembled a half-felled tree.

"You'll be thinking of going over?"

"Yes. I have business at the priory. An inquiry."

"Ahhh."

The cutpurse leaned over the edge of the water. Leaned so far the softest breeze or nudge would have set him swimming. Was reflecting on something for a while before he spoke what was on his mind.

"Mystical river, this. Magical they say. Old. Ancient. Some say it was sacred to the Druids. Sacred to the ones before them even. As far back as religion goes. Know what it means, Mersey?"

"Boundary River, I believe. It marks the old Mercia-Northumbria boundary."

"More than that, so the legends say." I pushed for an explanation. The cutpurse would not explain further. For the first time, I noticed his eyes were two different colours. One Brown. The other blue. It gave him an odd, unnerving appearance. I was not frightened.

"Land of folklore is this. Most of it is getting forgotten, but there's some of us still knows. You ever hear tell of The Green Knight? The Chapel of the Knight is said to be somewhere over yonder." He indicated across the river, where the most visible building was the sandstone of the priory spire.

"It is Birkenhead priory?" The cutpurse cackled. Mocking my stupidity. How was I to know otherwise?

"Nay lad. Nay. Further up, supposed to be. Towards Runcorn."

I began to divert him. Make conversation. Advance my enquiries. Seemed the sort of person who would know things.

"Speaking of green, in a manner. Tell me. Have you heard of Brother Greene who resides at the priory? He has information pertaining to my inquiry."

"No Brother Greene at the priory lad. Though I hear tell plenty have sought him, whoever he might be. Aye. I met some of them before they crossed over. Like you. Just said they had business with Brother Greene at the priory. Told them like I told you. No Brother Greene at the priory."

"Did any of them tell you what their business was?"

"No. Secretive they were. Suspicious. Shifty. Sly. The look a rich merchant has when he sees gold."

"They were greedy?"

"They were. But for what, I wonder?"

"A book," I say. "They were sent to Brother Greene by an old priest at Ravenglas."

"A book you say? How curious. How curious."

"A legendary grimoire. Scientia Universalis."

"Can't say I've ever heard of it but books are precious things. There are those who would kill for a book."

"There are. This is a book which is said to kill by its own accord. Tosh I suspect. I seek to know who, maybe what, really killed those men."

The cutpurse was still. Perhaps he was mistaken when he said he had not heard of the Scientia? He knew it by another name?

"Do you know of any books beside this Scientia

Universalis which could kill? Is there anything similar in local folklore?"

"Local folklore? Last dragon slain in England. Again at Runcorn. Place where Lucifer fell. Again. Runcorn. Last resting place of Thor's hammer…"

"Let me guess. Runcorn?"

"Nay. Thurstaton. On the Dee side of the peninsula. Anyhow. I know of many local folktales but no books which can kill."

"Thank you sir. You have been most helpful," I said. Gave him a sovereign.

Went on his way. I returned to watching the priory for a while afterwards.

The more I stared across the river, the more I was struck by the curious connection between those three folktales. All of them connected with Runcorn. Dragon could be easily dismissed but the remaining two could not. Had heard tell from my old tutor, the magnificent Marged Ferch Evans, that the Green Knight was an embodiment of Lucifer. Could be no coincidence the chapel of the Green Knight and this place where Lucifer fell, were reputed to be close to one another. There was also this name. Brother Greene. Too much of a coincidence this man whom nobody had heard of had a similar name to a figure from local folklore?

Was possible Brother Greene might be using the name to associate himself with the legend. Might have been an ordinary man living upriver. A madman who claimed to be the Green Knight. Also claimed to have the Scientia.

In this idea there was a possible explanation to the mystery. The confessors were not killed by the book. They were killed by Brother Greene recreating the legend of the knight. Challenging the confessors to kneel before him. Decapitating them. Perhaps saying that if they were worthy, his sword would pass clean through them without harm.

Yet… I had not heard mention of any confessors being decapitated. Would have done so before if it were the case. Perhaps Brother Greene was killing them by other means?

Either way, I could feel I was closing in on a rational truth behind the legend of the book. Behind the deaths. Behind the ambition, the lust of Father Heather.

Crossed the river the next day. Undertook enquiries at the priory. Predictably they knew nothing of Brother Greene. Others had come searching. I was not the first. Of course. After riding off in the direction of Runcorn those same others, almost inevitably, were found washed up on the shore at Eastham. Apart from that they had ridden towards Runcorn I learned little which was new.

Returned to Liverpool. Consulted a map of the river. I could not help but notice there was a clear channel downstream from Runcorn to Eastham. Depending on currents a body placed in the water at Runcorn could feasibly wash up again at Eastham. Added weight to my theory concerning Brother Greene murdering the men. Existence of Scientia Universalis was looking less likely. Eldrick be damned for yet again being proven correct. This appeared a most human form of evil.

Three days later, after spending time in Liverpool, going through the facts of the case, making further enquiries, coming to no new conclusions, I rode in the direction of Runcorn.

Easy enough journey. Indeed a blighted country of marshland. Bog. Fen. Not good for agriculture. I supposed fishing, the river, the sea, were the main source of livelihood.

Morning I set out, an eerie fog filtered through the marshes. Black crows circling ahead. Easy to see why this was a country of folklore. Superstition. The land lent itself well to stories of the ghoulish. Could have invented half a dozen stories on my ride to Runcorn. I wondered if it had not been on such a morning Sir John Stanley, most likely candidate for the Gawain poet, had come up with the idea for his own story.

By noon I was at a place called Elton. Stopped at a

tavern for sustenance. Further inquiries here too. Tavern keeper, Noah, asking to be named as 'Noah of Elton' if ever I told of my adventures, knew nothing of the confessors.

"Nobody come in here talking about a book. But then why would they, if they were after some special treasure? Not something you'd go blabbing about is it? Can't say I've heard about Brother Greene either. Nearest place you might find him is Birkenhead."

"They don't know him but they've heard of him because the confessors have been there asking after him."

"So what makes you think they came this way?"

"Their bodies were found washed up at Eastham. If they'd been placed in the waters at Runcorn..."

"Could have washed over from Hale point." I bit my lip. Shook my head.

"Don't think so. I think the current would have taken them further up."

Noah Of Elton pondered. He left the tavern in the care of his wife whilst he went off for ten minutes. Came back with a grey-bearded riverman. Smelled like he lived in the river. Regarded me with suspicion.

"What you want ey? Bodies at Eastham ey? Heard of them. Can't say it's odd. People drownses all the time in the river. Bad river she is. Bad. Legends say she's a passage into the underworld."

"If the bodies were washed up at Eastham where might they have come from?" The old man considered my question, began to trace the line of the river on the table.

"Depends which way the tide was going. Sefton. St Michaels. Close to Liverpool, if it was coming in. Sure. They come this way they might have crossed at Runcorn, ridden back along the other side. Aye. But..." He again traced the line of the river. "Weston Point. Just before the gap. Though every chance the outflow from the Weaver junction might push them over the other side. Or an incoming tide might pull them up the Weaver or into the Runcorn marshes."

"Nowhere else?"

"Only other place I could think of is Baden Point. Direct north. Why they'd go up there I don't know."

"Nothing up there," Noah of Elton added. "Just an island. Small outcrop at the end of a causeway."

"Any churches? Chapels? Buildings? Derelict settlements?"

"Not a thing. Well. There's a bit of an old cave sort of thing, but it's flooded most of the time."

Old cave? The chapel of The Green Knight was reputed to be inside of a cave.

No. Stupid. Silly. The Green Knight was a story made up by John Stanley when he was out riding in the fog. The idea there was a mortal man camped on the island waiting for somebody to show up looking for a legendary book stretched credulity. Even if he knew Father Heather was sure to send someone, why would he wait around on the chance?

Unless…

Monks at Birkenhead Priory were in on the conspiracy? Maybe the prior? Somebody shows up looking for Brother Greene. They're sent over land towards Baden Point whilst one of the monks takes the easy route by river. Waits at the island. Kills the confessor. Dumps their body in the water.

What purpose? What did the monks have to gain by murdering those who sought the Scientia? Why hadn't they sent me direct to the point? Had I been too much of an authority? An investigator? I had not hidden my intention so of course they would not direct me the same as they had the others. I was something to be kept at bay. Kept from the truth.

Yet… If it was the case the monks of Birkenhead Priory were luring people to Baden Point, then Baden Point had to be my next destination. I asked for a guide. Noah of Elton agreed to accompany me as far as the causeway. Would not go further. Said he would wait there, till nightfall for my return.

"Tis a blasted place," he said. "Can't think why anybody would go up there. You sure you won't reconsider?"

I did not reconsider.

The causeway. Snaking track of mud flanked by the black reeds of the Runcorn marshes. Reminded of Moses. The parting of the Red Sea. Imagined as I crossed the walls would come crashing down. Like the Egyptians I would be drowned. Horse had similar thoughts. Outright refused to cross.

Therefore, reluctantly, most uncomfortably, I trudged on foot through the boggy mud of the causeway. Took over an hour.

The other end. Open land. Nothing to care for. Flat with an expansive view of the low-tide river. Nothing but grey mud. Thought one more time how this was benighted country. Wet. Marshy. Unpleasant. Only feature of the island was the cave. Really a cleft in the ground. Sort of canyon. Short cliff preventing the Mersey water from flooding it completely. High tides would overwhelm the dam, flood the cave temporarily.

Therein another theory presented. Confessors had gone down into the cave. Drowned by the incoming tide. Bodies washed out again at following tide. Deposited at Eastham.

Then explain to me what all this was about Brother Greene? It was not a satisfying explanation. Unless, of course, there was no Brother Greene. He was a figment? A rouse? A convenient scapegoat for the tragic deaths of these men? Yet, again, why would the monks of Birkenhead send them here to die?

Only way I was to find the answer was to venture into the cave. Whether fate be foul or fair, why falter I, or fear? What should man do but dare? I dared.

Not without fear.

Cave entrance slippery. Greasy. Damp with river water. Easy to see how a man could go wrong. Break his leg. Back. Neck. Narrow enough you would certainly strike your head on the stones if you fell. Foot goes from under you. Feel the sensation of falling. Don't even notice when your mangled body comes to rest at the bottom of the cave. It was deeper than it looked. Twenty feet? Not difficult to get down. Not something an inexperienced climber might manage with ease. I wondered what the geology of this thing was. Sinkhole? Why a sinkhole here? No. Not sinkhole. Ancient mine? Cut into the sediment at the bedrock. Rocks worn down by years of the river coming in. Out. Deeper than twenty feet once. Thirty forty deep deep mine.

Down deeper. Felt like I was starting to swim. Air around me thin but breathable. Rocks. Slimy. Greasy. Mersey dripping ditch water. Foul nasty dripping cesspit shit-smelly Mersey ditch water. Thin trickle from above. Silence. Not even sparrows.

Brace myself over sharp drop. Slide. Nearly fall. Nearly break my leg. Would the tide fill this hole? Might take time. Subsequent tides would fill it further. But then where did the water go go go go go?

Thoughts echo back to me me me me me. Strange -ange -ange -ange. Not even speaking -eaking -eaking -eaking. Yet yet yet yet. Now no light above -ove -ove -ove. Gone gone gone gone gone. Down further -urther -urther.

Can't see. Can't see handholds. Where I'm placing my feet. Too precarious to fumble for a light. Lost my hat. Knocked off by a jutty rock.

Voices. Lottsa voices. Inside my head? Outside? Hi! Who are you? Dunno. Who's speaking? Dunno? What's going on? Dunno. Downy down down down down ha ha ha ha ha ha ha ha ha. Leap child Aurelius. Leap Leap. Ha ha ha ha. How you know his name Brother? I don't. I do. Maybe it is his name maybe it isn't. SHUT UP SOME OF US ARE TRYING TO SLEEP. Hark at her ducky. It's daylight love. Sleep at night when the tide comes in. Who are you are you are you are you? More to the point who are you? Dunno. Dunno. Dunno. Dunno. Head. Thought. No thought Something in the air? Can feel it. Entering lungs. Smog. Toxin. Toxteth toxin ducky. Gets us all at first. Watch ya step now. Ooop. There we go. Y'alright?

Stopped to rest.

Tiring.

Exhausted.

Not sure why.

"Fine, thank you," I said. No ethereal voice answered back. No echo.

Again I braced myself against the walls. Closed my eyes. What in hell was this cave? No wonder the others hadn't come out alive if there was some sort of gas down here, screwing with their heads. Suspected might be the case.

Looked up again. No light. Might be impossible to climb back out.

Climb bonny lad down into this hole never again see the sun. Something not normal here. Slowing. Pushing through a wall of aspic. Gelatine. Has gelatine been invented yet? Yes yes it has, do people eat aspic in my century? What about George Formby? What's the point? Heh heh turned out nice again. Get to the bottom as quick as you like. Oh you're a top yeah so am I fancy a smooch mate? God save Queen Victoria she really hates your mam!!!! They call her Queen Victoria she takes it up the bum! No I don't know what's going on either but isn't this fun boys et seagulls?

Oh well can't stay around here chatting all day can we? Bye bye everybody bye bye....

Feet touched sandy ground. Bottom of the cave. Head cleared of all inexplicable chaos. Could breathe again. Paused to enjoy the taste. Felt like I had been coming down for years. Not minutes.

Dark here. Pitch. Shuddering. Air cold. Damp. Wrapped my arms around myself. Thought I might be going mad. Climb down had felt like I was going mad. Or maybe I had slipped? This was a comatose dream?

Kept clinging to the thought that all that noise was the result of some noxious gas or I was lying comatose at the bottom of the cave. Was doubt in my mind though. Uncertainty. Everything which had been in my head a moment before felt more real than anything I had ever felt. World above river marsh back through Elton Birkenhead Liverpool up north to Ravenglas down south to London then to Abermaw. Everything past, everything which had led me here – it seemed as though that were the comatose dream.

I was motionless in the blackness at the bottom of the cave for some time. Don't know how long.

Blackness, eventually pinpricked by a green light. Grew. Light grew around me. Like a trailing plant. An ivy. Found myself lifted up. Placed, as if by a group of hidden bearers, into a soft chair. Felt warm now. Relaxed. At peace. Like I was being caressed. Loved.

Music. Soft. Sweet. Gentle music about the stars. The moon. A man floating amongst them. I can't recall a thing about the song other than that.

I closed my eyes. Listened. Imagined I was the man floating amongst the stars. I could see it all crystal clear. Could the see the Earth. Oh beautiful blue Earth. Colourful speck in an endless void of oblivion.

Opened my eyes. Seated in a parlour beside a roaring fireplace. There was a man seated opposite. Watching me. Smiling. Something sinister in his smile. One of his eyes brown. The other blue. The cutpurse I had met in Liverpool. From a window behind him, green light flooded the room, bathing him with a natural aura. An aura which gave the impression he had sprang from the soil when the earth was young.

"You are most welcome here," he said. "Would you care for tea? Coffee? Posca? It is an ancient Roman beverage I developed a liking for some time ago. Here. Try some."

A glass of pale liquid appeared beside me.

"No. Thank you, all the same."

"Oh, come now. Is it not rude to refuse a drink when it is served to you? I thought from our meeting the other day you were of kinder heart?"

"If it is all the same, Brother Greene, for that is who I am assuming you are, all I would like is an explanation. For the deaths?"

"Ahhh. Scientia Universalis. Yes. You came seeking answers did you not? It sets you apart from the others. They foolishly came seeking the book. You are, may I say, a wiser man, Sir Aurelius. You wish to know what the Scientia really is? I shall be brief. There is so little time and you must be returned to the human plain. It is an idea. Nothing more. Something formed in the mind of man aeons ago. A book which could never be read. Over time, legends grew around it. It became the Scientia Universalis you have heard of. The book which kills when it is read by the unworthy. But it does not exist. It never existed. There is no book, Sir Aurelius."

"So what killed those men?"

Brother Greene offered no answer, but I saw it in his eyes. As he had done with myself, he had approached the confessors in Liverpool in order to divine their intentions. Finding they sought Scientia, he drew himself against them. Made a subtle suggestion regarding The Green Knight, waited for them to inevitably come here to his chapel. Took their souls as his payment for what they wanted.

What he was I never worked out. Demon spirit? Devil? Living embodiment of the Green Knight? I never asked. I did not wish to know. Still do not. It is better that way.

"A better question would be to ask why they had to die. Simple. Elementary. Knowledge. It was knowledge. What the Buddhist refers to as nirvana. The knowledge said to be contained within the book. Knowledge of what lies beyond the skin of the universe. In seeking Scientia, they really sought the knowledge within. They had to make a payment for that."

"As a punishment? A warning to others?"

Brother Greene started to chuckle.

"Neither. The payment was death. Their soul. Death is

the only way any mortal can obtain the knowledge of Scientia Universalis. It is not knowledge which life can give. A living man will only ever see small parts. The only way to see the whole is to pass beyond the mortal plain. To pass into the unknown."

> Lay your breath upon a candle flame,
> Softly, sweetly, speak my name.
> With one swift kiss sing death's refrain,
> To cast me from this mortal plain.

A simple explanation. Those confessors sought Scientia Universalis. A book which does not exist. A legend. A mere idea Brother Greene gave them what was said to be contained within. The only way he could. By placing his breath upon their flame, speaking their name. It was not the knowledge they really wanted. They wanted the book. Only the book, and not even for themselves. They wanted the book for Father Heather. Father Heather was the one who truly desired the knowledge within. Father Heather, who would not, for whatever reason, journey so short a distance to claim it for his own. Brother Greene could not give the book to those who sought him out. Instead he gave them what was contained within. As a consolation.

I grieved. How callous, how cruel and needless a chain of suffering this was. I don't believe Brother Greene was evil. Not so evil as Father Heather.

No, he was not evil, but he was not kind either. A kind spirit would have warned those seekers that they must die to obtain that knowledge.

Father Heather still wanted that knowledge, though. So I returned to Ravenglas and gave him what he wanted. I took my lesson from Brother Greene. Be unkind. Do not tell him there is only one way to acquire what he seeks. Let him find out for himself when he opens the book. Strokes the page. Unknowingly let the poison I had coated there enter his skin.

I murdered him. I snuffed out his light like a breath

upon a candle flame.

We strolled from the church, taking the air before we rode south.

"What do you intend to do with the book?" Eldrick asked.

"Return it to where it belongs," I said. "Return it to hell."

A coy smile crossed Eldrick's face.

"I assume by hell you mean this Brother Greene at Birkenhead?"

"I don't think I need to go so far. I will throw it into the waters at Liverpool. It will reach him. Then I shall return to Abermaw. I shall tell old Victor why his son died."

"What will you tell him, Brother?"

I remembered another old song. Part of a Norse skald's epic, which tells of how Odin sacrificed his eye at Mimir's Well.

Knowledge, wisdom, for you will see,
Is not a blessing at all.
An addiction at worst. The mightiest thirst.
But most of all, dear nephew, a curse.

I would tell Victor that John had been gifted another man's curse. A curse he did not deserve but which had, at last, been given to the correct person.

One's For Sorrow

Imogen Morgan

For Alice and Danny, who made sorrowful times happier.

A cawing rung through the air. The woman fell.

The bird was relentless in its attack. Its eyes gleamed; talons scored deep lines across her pregnant stomach. As panicked bystanders rushed to her aid, the winged creature opened its beak and darkness enveloped her vision.

~

"How have you been doing recently, Vera?"

"Um – yeah. Been doing okay."

The counsellor's face morphed into a mask of relaxed formality. Her voice drifted off into the distance as, from the corner of her eye, Vera spied a magpie out in the courtyard. One's for sorrow, she thought…

"Have you had any more of those thoughts we discussed last time?"

Her voice cut through Vera's wandering thoughts like a match being struck.

"Um…yes. A couple of times." She swallowed. "Just about the birds again. A-and my daughter. They, um, attack her, and then turn on me."

The counsellor blinked, clicking between tabs on her computer. Each click made Vera wince. She rattled off about further referrals and how, yes, ornithophobia was a very real thing that affected lots of people and how Vera wasn't alone… blah blah blah. Same old spiel.

As she left the building, Vera saluted the magpie. It cawed loudly in her face before flying off. Shaking, she got into her car.

~

The creature shook its feathered coat and lunged at her. Vera screamed, falling backward onto the bedroom floor. It jabbed its mangled beak into the bedclothes, catching her by the throat and drawing blood –

She seized the bedside lamp and slammed it into the bird's neck.

When she came to, the lamp lay broken halfway across the room. A shattered porcelain vase lay a few metres away from it. Her hands flew to her throat, finding it unblemished. There were no signs of a struggle apart from the mess caused by the thrown lamp.

"What. The Fuck."

She got up shakily. Before leaving, she turned to face the very much undisturbed room in disbelief.

In the shattered glass remnants of the lamp lay a feather.

Surely not. Surely the episode was over – everything else was untouched, after all. Vera's heart was hammering so hard she swore the room was pulsing in time with it.

"I-I've got to get upstairs."

The room swam. Waves of rose-printed wallpaper came crashing against her head in a sickly rhythm.

Desperate, she fumbled with her mobile. The waves grew more intense – she knew she needed to get upstairs, to get into a safe space so that she could ride out this panic. She knew she could do it, but she couldn't get this bloody phone to work; everything in her room was laughing at her, and her heart was about to crawl out of her mouth and her hands were too sweaty and she kept mistyping her ex-husband's number of all people and for God's sake Vera, why can't you do anything right, you useless cow –

Something hit the floor upstairs.

Vera stilled. Her eyes bulged as she looked up at the ceiling. The attic was the only room above hers – her daughter's room. And Nellie was at school... wasn't she? The noise had changed now, like something was rolling across the floor. It stopped after a few seconds and... shattered? Vera couldn't place it, but it reminded her of the wet crunch of breaking an eggshell.

Fear seized her. She raced towards the attic door and wrenched the ladder down. Whatever was up there could have hurt Nellie and Vera swore, if something had happened to her, she wouldn't be able to forgive herself. Gasping for breath, she opened the door and –

Nothing.

~

The sounds of children gleefully shouting resonated across the park. Vera took a deep breath before getting out of her car. She was here for Nellie, but she knew all the other mothers were here, which meant they would undoubtedly make their sickeningly sweet jabs at her and her family. Vera hated them – their stupidly big cars, their smoothies, their Zumba classes. Mostly just how they looked at her. Like she was the shit on their very expensive shoes.

As she got out of the car, she could see a pack of them by the sidelines. One of them caught her eye, and suddenly they were strutting towards her like a pack of vultures. So much for avoiding them.

"Hello ladies!" said Vera genially. They drawled their responses, mostly just looking her up and down, assessing her like a cut of meat. "H-how are you all?"

"Fine, darling – how are you?" asked Antonia.

Antonia was the head of the school's 'Governors and Friends' scheme. She had a habit of being particularly cruel to Vera.

"I'm alright, yeah. Um. Been better, but, uh – yeah."

Antonia gave her a dead smile that didn't reach her eyes. It struck Vera then how uncanny it was that all the women were smiling at her in the exact same way. Like a pack of wolves. Or a flock of birds.

"I've come to see Nellie play!" She laughed nervously. "I love watching her have fun."

Something in Antonia's face shifted then. Her eyebrows relaxed into a frown before smoothing imperceptibly out again. One of the women went to whisper to her friend, but a sharp glance from Antonia stopped her.

"Well, darling. We'll leave you to watch her then." She led the gaggle of women away from Vera, who stood surprised at Antonia's lack of sugar-coated insult. Before she turned to the game, she saw Antonia's eyes glistening with tears in the sunlight.

~

Six weeks after her previous appointment, Vera rang her therapist's office for her scheduled advanced treatment assessment.

"And you've said in previous questionnaires that these behaviours are caused by an attack – if you're comfortable, do you mind elaborating, please, love?"

Vera swallowed. A photo of her and Toby on the mantelpiece caught her eye. They stood on a pier, one hand each on her pregnant belly. He was kissing her forehead.

"Um – a bird attacked me when I was heavily pregnant. I went into premature labour. My counsellor thinks I have ornithophobia – the, um, fear of birds – as a result."

Outside, the sky darkened. Leaves fluttered in the wind, rippling through the air without intent or malice. The therapist on the phone spoke to Vera about a referral for individual psychotherapy before ending the call. As Vera sat down with a cup of tea, a familiar scraping began from upstairs. She turned up the radio, trying to ignore the curl of panic in her gut.

~

The birds circled her, cackling, engulfing her with their wings. Vera tried to scream, but a talon raked down her face and into her mouth, cutting into the flesh of her cheek. One beak pinned her by the forearm to the blood-soaked carpet. Then the other arm. Another bird reared its great head and let out a great cry, a cry of war, a cry of killing, before striking through Vera's right calf, with another bird doing the same on her left, so that she was prone on the ground. She couldn't even scream. She wanted to scream for someone, Toby, Nellie – Nellie! Somewhere upstairs she could hear her baby girl screaming for help. She began to struggle against the beaks, but they held fast through skin and muscle.

Then, they started pecking.

~

Vera gasped awake. She sat up immediately – no holes in her arms or legs. No bleeding. Just another episode. Just another episode.

Her hand found the mug on her bedside table. A sunny yellow colour, the handle's paint had been worn away like limestone. The tea was hours old, probably made last night as a soother before bed. Lemon and ginger tickled Vera's nose as she adjusted her sitting position, bracing her hand underneath her as she gently flexed her foot.

Wait.

The carpet was wet. Her hand was covered in blood.

She sat up. The blood couldn't have been hers – obviously, she didn't have any wounds. But blood was seeping through the carpet onto her clothes. Something sharp pricked her hand – a feather shaft. In panic, she scrambled to her feet.

"One…Two…Three…" Vera tried to control her breathing, countless titbits from her therapist running through her head. "Four… Five… Six…"

"One…Two…Three…"

Then she heard it.

"Mummy?"

Vera gasped. Nellie was at school. Or –or with Toby today.

"Mummy?"

"Darling?" It was coming from the kitchen. Running downstairs, she became aware of another sound. A low droning sound – voices? Vera wanted to cry, but she had to be strong, she had to be strong so Nellie wasn't scared.

"Sweetheart, where are you? Nellie?!"

"What's that on the horizon, Mummy?"

Through the glass doors in the kitchen, Vera saw a great black mass in the sky. A writhing, screaming thing. It seemed so far away, like a nightmare just awoken from, yet Vera could make out the unmistakable shape of flapping wings.

And all at once, they descended.

A thousand birds came thundering through the glass doors, shouting their dreadful song. Wings and beaks and feathers connected with the glass, shattering it instantly. The heavy, wet stench of blood soured the air as the cacophony stopped as suddenly as it had occurred, leaving Vera to peer through her fingers at the mess of bird and gore now congealing on her kitchen floor.

Her fingers found her phone.

"Toby? Toby?! Help me, I – I need you."

"Vera? I told you not to call me. We've been over this."

"I know, I'm sorry – it's out of hours and I don't know who else to –"

"I'm at work."

"This whole fucking cloud of birds just flew into the kitchen! There's glass and blood everywhere and their wings are all snapped, Toby! Their talons look exactly like the ones on that bird that attacked me d-do you remember? All white and sharp."

"Vera."

"And Toby. I heard Nellie! She was upstairs o-or something I, I couldn't find her, but I hear—"

"Shut up! Just fucking shut up for once!"

Vera's voice died in her throat. She had grown accustomed to Toby's reticence in the final weeks of their marriage, but this anger was an entirely new beast. She heard him quietly excuse himself over the phone as he presumably got up to leave his desk.

"Vera. You cannot keep doing this. You have to accept she's gone."

"I...don't understand." Vera trailed off. She felt too light, like she was swimming in hot air.

"I know you think Nellie's still here. But she's dead, Vera. And I – I don't understand if this is a sick joke that you keep playing on me, but it's got to stop."

The disconnection tone signified he had hung up, yet Vera still clutched the phone as if it would give her some semblance of stability.

Silence crept into the room. The dead birds gazed up at her, glassy-eyed. One of them shuddered violently, like it was having a seizure. It lay still before heaving itself up to crouch in front of Vera, clutching the sides of her face with ragged fingertips.

Whatever this was, she thought, whatever mad fucked up thing this was, it had to be real. Her daughter had died, and that was real. She hadn't thought it was. How could she? Her darling girl was dead! That ache, that violence from which Nellie's death came, that was real. It hadn't stopped chasing her after that – it must still be hungry, she thought. She looked at the creature on the ground, and rage spread across her skin like burning flames.

"What do you want from me?" she uttered. "What the fuck do you want from me?"

As if in response, the bird dragged its white talon once along the floor. Again. Again. Again.

Upstairs, something began shuffling about. Once again, Vera heard the crunching of eggshells underfoot, followed by a slow creaking of- was that bedsprings?

That was Nellie's room.

"I know you think Nellie's still here. But she's dead, Vera."

The bird finished its etching.

"Come upstairs, Mummy."

~

Toby slammed the car door shut. As much as he didn't want to see Vera, something in the tone of her voice unsettled him. It reminded him of the final days of their marriage: she kept telling him there was something upstairs, that it was Nellie getting up, or playing with her dolls. He was glad he'd left in the end. But for all his anger towards her, the loss of their daughter was one they shared.

Third key on the ring. He had kept it – just in case.

Nothing in him could have been ready for the sight of the house.

Vera was right.

Oh god.

He followed a trail of bloodied prints through the kitchen. Vera's, obviously, but there was another set next to hers. Mismatched, long claws extending at odd angles, digging into the wood, the carpet. Up the staircase, now ripped to shreds.

She wasn't in the bedroom. She wasn't anywhere on the first floor.

He took a deep breath and pulled the attic door down.

The smell hit him first. A tang of sweat and dust, filling his nose like spores. His foot connected with something smooth, and he jumped back.

Immense shards of eggshell jutted from the floorboards. Mucus coated each piece, congealed like old spit. Tinges of blood made the globules look as though there were veins running through them. Like a foetus. It was spattered on every surface. A bird with strangely white talons lay in a pile of blankets with its head ripped off.

Then Toby saw Nellie's old cot. His mouth opened in a scream, but what he saw was too wrong for his voice to grace his surroundings, even in terror.

In the cot lay a creature. It had its back to him, but he could see its feathers. They were mussed and fluffy – it had to be a chick, yet it was huge. It stirred in its sleep, shifting a feathered limb.

And as his legs gave out beneath him and all went dark, he saw Vera sleeping as the chick wrapped its wing around her, pulling its mother in closer.

Supernova

Imogen Morgan

For my parents, who have watched me grow since I was but a sapling.

[PREFACE/COMP5670 - This report has been revised and submitted by Doctor Saborova's supervisor following the results of the experiment.]
[Report begins below.]

Report of Dr Karanya Saborova: Experimentation on the effects of light on the Supernova plant.

Abstract:
  This experiment will aim to determine the effect of light intensity on the rate of growth of the Supernova plant.

[Please note: this abstract has been revised since the experiment took place. Much of the material has been redacted due to repetition and, in some cases, incomprehensibility.]

Introduction:

The Supernova plant was first discovered by Doctor Venkatamara Singh in 2021. Little evidence has yet been produced regarding the plant's life cycle or digestive nature; however, initial studies by Dr Singh suggest it photosynthesises in part. Rather than requiring water and carbon dioxide, Singh's findings suggest that the Supernova plant requires only sunlight and grows at a heightened rate compared to that of known plant species. Dr Singh's investigations concluded that the Supernova grows fastest when exposed to an extreme light source; however, his results regarding why are inconclusive. One notable thing absent from Dr Singh's research is a reason for the name 'Supernova plant'.

The Supernova plant has yet to be examined in laboratory conditions. Thus, the Supernova's growth rate relative to light exposure will be measured within laboratory conditions, as per Dr Singh's research. I will be measuring it against a control in order to ensure any findings are accurate to my variable, in this case, light. My chosen control will thus be darkness. I will measure the growth rate of one Supernova plant left in complete darkness, and one exposed to sunlight during the day and light-emitting diodes during the night. The chambers in which the plants are contained will be vacuum sealed to prevent any carbon dioxide or water affecting the experiment as external variables.

The experiment will be recorded as an actual-time observational report.

Method:

Day 1:
Plants are at their initial sapling size of about 4 inches. The plants have been designated the names Zero and One. Both plants are being kept in the same vacuum-sealed chamber to ensure they have access to the same temperature and air composition; Zero is sectioned off and kept in complete darkness, whereas One is constantly exposed to sunlight and L.E.Ds by way of a revolving soil tray that follows the path of the light throughout the day and night. Light intensity ranges between 70,000 to 90,000 lux when measured with a light meter.

Week 1:
One has achieved a height of 13.5 inches. This is resultant of a constant exposure to minimum 70,000 lux 24 hours a day. Zero has remained approximately 4 inches in height. No gas or water has contaminated One's progress.

One has sprouted a mass of roots around its base. They appear to be unlike typical plants in that the roots are external and negatively hydrotropic and geotropic. They appear to be growing towards Zero.

Week 2:
One's roots have reached the separation between it and Zero. This root growth is yet unexplainable.

One has meanwhile reached a height of 30 inches with constant exposure to minimum 70,000 lux 24 hours a day. Zero has maintained a height of 4 inches. Zero's body appears to be etiolated and dying.

Week 3:
One's roots have extended beneath the separation barrier. One notable concern is how One avoided breaking through the barrier and instead grew underneath. If the barrier had been broken, light

contamination would hypothetically have occurred and the effect of darkness on Zero could not be efficiently measured.

Week 3, Day 4:
One's roots have burst through the soil bed containing Zero. There is no discernible tropism that One is either adhering to or avoiding.

One has reached a height of 51.5 inches. The roots at its base have swollen and become bulbous and pulsate at a rate of 3bpm. The roots around Zero's base are identical.

Week 3, Day 6:
Zero's condition has exacerbated. One's roots have burrowed inside Zero's base. Now Zero is pulsing in time with One's roots. The pulse rate has increased to 31bpm. The cause of the pulsing is yet unknown.

One has reached a height of 70 inches. Zero remains withered.

Both plants have achieved a colour change from black to purplish red. The colour intensifies with each pulse.

Week 4, Day 1:
The pulsing in each plant has increased to 73bpm.

Rather than growing in height, One has become swollen and expanded in width by approximately 3 inches, as have its roots. Zero has become equally swollen.

Week 4, Day 2;
The pulsing in each plant has extremified to 186bpm.

One and Zero have grown a bulb-like head of about 9.7 and 9.2 inches respectively. These heads change dramatically in colour whenever the plants pulse, suggesting a reaction or a change of some kind is occurring within.

Week 4, Day 3:

I do not have quite the words to be able to describe what has occurred since my last observation, yet I know in a dutiful capacity I must try.

One and Zero have... exploded. The pulsing increased to an immeasurable extent, before the bulb heads swelled within mere seconds, and burst open. Unidentifiable plant matter contaminated the walls of the laboratory space and covered the outside of my vacuum suit. The heads glowed a bright aching purple before they ruptured. The matter is of a deep black colour and feels sticky to the touch.

As an educated guess, I believe the swelling of the roots and the bulb heads was a preparatory implosion before the external rupture. Perhaps the plants are leguminous.

Zero's body is destroyed. The matter expelled from both the Supernova plants has eaten away at its body. Active, quickened signs of decomposition are visible.

I now believe I understand the reasoning behind the name Supernova.

Week 4, Day 6:

I had believed the experiment to be over following the previous observation. I was wrong. I apologise for the personal interjection, but I feel it is relevant.

My skin is itchy. There are dark blotches all over my body. When examining the video log footage, I observed that the ruptured material had pulped itself on my suit in a pattern that matches the blotches on my skin. I examined my suit and there are holes matching the pattern. I do not know what this means.

The roots around One have regrown. They are now growing in the direction of my observation booth.

Week 5, Day 1:

My skin is hard where the dark patches are. I can feel lumps in my flesh. They're seed pods. They must be. Growing deep into my skin, tissue, organ, bone. Itching is incessant. It goes beyond any knowable pain: it's the pain of knowing something is changing, growing inside of you, for that is what it must be...surely. The roots are at the door of the booth now.

Something is calling to me, deep within.

And I am scared to answer.

Week 5, Day 3:
They're sprouting.

The roots loom outside the glass door, bright and aching. I can feel the seed pods pulsing within me – connective, epithelial, nervous, muscle. Down deep through epidermis, dermis, hypodermis.

I think it needs me alive to grow and reproduce. Like a parasite. Or a host.

It has rooted inside my bones.

They itch.

Week 5, Day 4:
3i29p23i258u0fb323333333333333333,,,,error,,,,Cann ot,,,,type. Motttttttor controlllllllllll losttttttt.

```
[Note: this entry was transcribed from an
audio format.]
```

The roots sing to the seeds deep within my body and the seeds sing back. I do not want them to. I cannot think. The seeds pulse and spots of red heat spread across my skull. The song is loud, and I can feel myself giving in to its deep, wet voice.

I do not want to. The seeds bloom inside me and the pain is fertile, dark and sticky.

Week 5, Final Day:
[No data available]

Conclusion:

The results of this experiment are ambiguous. No consistent conclusion is apparent. Officially, the experiment was inconclusive and a failure.

Dr Saborova's whereabouts are indiscernible. Her laboratory walls were covered with organic matter; however, due to the nature of their presentation, they are unfit for analysis. Much of it, however, resembled human bodily residue. Interestingly, the presumed human residue has begun to decay.

There was another substance coating the walls of the laboratory. We have yet to identify it. It is dark and sticky in appearance.

The roots of the plants had burst through the glass partition between the lab space and the observational space. There is a dark patch on the floor in the centre of the observation space. An educated guess would be that this patch correlates with the dark sticky mass coating the walls. There are dark spots appearing in the residue that correlate the other substance.

The condition or whereabouts of the plant are unknown.

[Report ends/COMP5670]

The Doorman

Ben Fitzsimons

> *For Luna, who didn't contribute to this story at all and refused to proof-read anything. Thanks for not being too chatty while I write. You're a good dog.*

On the day he had received employment, The Doorman had only been thirteen years old. A passer-by dressed in outrageous finery had walked up to him, and plainly asked if he'd like to earn five pounds. All that would be required of him would be to stand passively by the entrance of a run-of-the-mill block of flats for one week, before reporting back everything he had seen. He would open the door as people approached, and say 'Good morning', or 'Good evening', depending on the time of day.

The only other guidance given was that he should, 'Never interfere. Never. You'll lose this as soon as you get involved.' As they said this, their hands waved the five-pound note alluringly in the newly employed Doorman's face, spraying spittle down upon him. When looking at their new employer, the boy found it difficult to remember where he was meant to be going; if he was headed home, or perhaps towards school. He put aside these questions and took the note.

So, The Doorman stood there, taking mental notes of the various profiles of downturned faces passing by as they left the building, before matching them to the opposing profiles as they slowly returned home. Occasionally they would glance noncommittally up at him, before turning their heads back down at the first sign of their gaze being met. The closest he ever got to conversation with the tenants were the vague grunts of gratitude sometimes given to him as he opened the door for them, which sustained him more than he would have cared to admit at the time.

He quickly gathered that if he were to have anything to report back to his employer at the end of the week, it would be the information he could extract from the residents' conversations.

'She got locked out again you know? She keeps claiming it's her being scatty, but I'm pretty certain her man is changing the locks. Somehow the locksmith keeps letting her back in. I bet I know how too.'

'Oh hello dear, how's your ma doing? I'll send him round to have another look at her when he gets back from the surgery. No, of course we wouldn't charge you. Not a penny until she's better.'

'You know that man who moved in across the hall from me? I keep hearing these noises. He seems a very pleasant man, I suppose, just a bit odd. I see this woman leaving his sometimes, but I've never seen how she gets in.'

These snippets slowly built a sort of internal map of the complex in his head, without the need to ever actually go further inside than the foyer. An overheard mention of a banging noise upstairs, or a lost cat with an address on its collar. All of this contributed to the labyrinthian mess of hallways he concluded must be present, if the information he had picked up was to make any sense at all. New comments or previously unseen residents would occasionally appear throughout the week, and each time they would either confirm or disprove one of The Doorman's working theories on the structure of the block.

In the entire week, there was only one time that The Doorman really considered offering his assistance to any of the residents. A young couple had passed him, both of them crying into each other in a way which made them appear as one unified sobbing mess. They staggered into the building as if they had been wounded, but they had no clear marks on them. Instinctively, he went to ask if they were alright, before the words of his employer made him pivot to simply wishing them a good evening. They both halted, now staring synchronously at him in a way which assured him that not only was it not a good evening, but that it seemed there were no more good evenings to be had. This was the first thing The Doorman shared with the employer as they returned the next week.

'A pity.' The distaste had rolled out of their mouth easier than the words.

Both of them stood looking at the other expectantly, before The Doorman realised that there was nothing else to be said on the subject. No help to be offered. Upon the conclusion of his report, the employer gave the boy a look adjacent to being impressed. They offered him another week of employment, this time for six pounds. Eagerly, the boy took them up on this chance, pleased by both the pay raise and the opportunity to check if the couple were okay.

During the next week, the couple (who he had now nicknamed Lucy and Ricky) didn't emerge from their flat for several days. Other people passed through the building, but where he had found their chatter easy to take note of before, it was now dull and extremely unmemorable.

'He's feeling much (better?) now is he love? (That's lovely to hear?) I'll send someone round to have a chat about settling up. (I'm sure it won't be much?)'

'He threw all her rubbish out into the hallway the other day. She just sat there in that hallway (trashy amongst trash?). (I made her a cuppa and asked if she wanted to come in for a bit?)'

'So you'll never guess who that woman leaving his flat was. Let's just put it this way, I don't have to worry about another woman, and I'm surprised he knows how to walk in those things. (If you can call him a 'he'?)'

By the time the couple did leave, their entire demeanour had changed. Ricky even slid a crisp note into The Doorman's palm as he walked past as a tip, and beat him to wishing them a good morning.

In fact, he was informed that he should 'Have the best day.'

They still walked unified as a single figure, but this time it was due to their arms being firmly wrapped around their respective waists. They burst into the outside world, giggling and chattering to each other with the kind of gossip that at best, nobody would find interesting, and at worst, they would find deeply annoying.

After this, the week flew by, a series of vignettes as the couple would burst back into his life, brightening it through his mere association to their ecstasy. By the time Lucy was rolling Ricky Jr back into the building, The Doorman was earning quite the considerable wage. His employer had continued to offer the same pay raise of a pound a week, as long as he continued his reports. This had really built up over nine months. The employer had taken particular interest in Lucy's pregnancy, which The Doorman had found sweet. They reverted to their dejected demeanour after they'd glimpsed the baby passing by.

They turned back to The Doorman and whispered, 'Not that one, but maybe the next.' This was shared as if it was self-explanatory, and The Doorman nodded along sympathetically whilst receiving his wage.

The child was remarkable. There was no real evidence to suggest this; The Doorman was too young to have spent enough time around babies to compare their quality. Regardless, he found himself impulsively attached to the child, even just through the glimpses he caught as Lucy and Ricky passed through with a pram.

The couple both worked, meaning that one day Lucy appeared before The Doorman with an almost frenzied look.

'I don't really know you, but I have to get to work. Ricky will be home in a couple of hours. His boss is keeping him longer than he said he would. It's a real problem. Could you watch him for a while?'

He nodded, deciding not to assure her that he had been watching him for longer than she knew. So, this was how he spent what turned out to be the next six hours, contentedly watching the child as he crawled and ate and blubbered. Residents raised their eyebrows as they went past. The Doorman realised that to them it must have looked like a child who was caring for a child, but he had worked more in the past year than many of them had in their lives.

'That's the young couple's kid. The ones in 4D. A very cute baby. Imagine leaving him to go off who knows where. Shameful.'

This childcare became somewhat of a pattern for The Doorman, and by the time Ricky Jr was going to school, they'd built quite the rapport. His parents worked random shifts, so over time it was often the case that The Doorman was the first face Ricky Jr saw most mornings. By the time he was graduating high school, the pair were on terms that The Doorman might have even dared to call friendly. This was the one thing that was never reported back to his employer, as he was aware they would not have approved.

Ricky Jr (now just Rick) left to attend university, and The Doorman pretended to be happy for him.

The Doorman

Eventually, when Lucy and Ricky were no longer present, Rick moved back into the flat block. His hairline was beginning to recede, and he only nodded as he passed by the front entrance to the building. The two men's eyes would meet occasionally, and the younger of the two would look at The Doorman with the vague familiarity of someone who thinks they might have seen you once or twice.

'Terrible what happened to those two. Just awful. Truly heart-breaking.'

'Awful what happened to those two. Just heart-breaking. Truly terrible'

'Heart-breaking what happened to those two. Just terrible. Truly awful.'

Then, without warning, she moved into 4C. She and Rick began to move in unison, just as his parents had done before him. They were always a step or two out of time with each other, but The Doorman was just pleased to see Rick talking to someone other than his colleagues through that brick of a Motorola. Before, she would whisper things in Rick's ear as they walked past, and he would embody laughter. Then, they began to stagger together like wounded animals, just as Rick's parents had done before him.

On several occasions The Doorman saw her walking alongside his employer, but he decided to dismiss any concerns out of a vague sense of loyalty and confidentiality. The glimpses of those walks were the only times he saw his employer grin in the whole time he was under them. She shook their hand, and soon the shipments of prams and cots began to arrive at the front desk.

In fact, such an excessive quantity of childcare equipment arrived at the foyer one morning, that The Doorman made his first and last trip into the main body of the building in order to deliver the parcels. The apartment complex was structured in a way which was, disappointingly, exceedingly ordinary. The décor didn't look like it had been updated in the decades since The Doorman's arrival; peeling gilding lined powder blue walls. Ornate mirrors appeared after each door, which he pretended not to see, as he did not like to overthink the implications of his own reflection.

A few months later, there was a new baby in the building. She came up to The Doorman and asked if he could watch them, and he agreed out of pure nostalgia. The same judgemental glares came from passing residents, who could still only see him as a child. He didn't really care; at this point he could remember most of them from when they were children themselves. Once or twice, he was asked if he was the son of the boy who used to work here when they were younger, as he looked exactly like him. He would always refute this without explanation.

The new child was a welcome addition to his life, bringing some variation and unpredictability. Unlike the people in the building, the child had no obvious motivation or predictable patterns. Most of all, The Doorman loved their lack of cynicism, which was an attribute that had become all too commonly observed in the building. They were so interested in everyone who came past, asking The Doorman reems of questions about all of the building's residents.

'Why?'

'Why did they do that?'

'Why did they speak like that?'

The Doorman had been so caught up with what the building's residents were doing, that the why of it all had never even taken shape as a passing thought. The child would look at him with expectant eyes every time they asked the question, but The Doorman only ever found one reasonable answer, which he gave consistently.

'Because they don't know anyone is watching.'

On the child's thirteenth birthday, The Doorman had

been left to care for them, as their mother had run out particularly distraught and in a hurry. His employer moved in to receive their weekly report, and their eyes pulsed on receiving the news that it was the child's birthday.

'Don't interfere.'

They moved towards the child and asked them if they would like to earn some pocket money at the apartment building across the road. Eagerly, the child went with them, hand in hand.

For years to follow, The Doorman would make absent-minded small talk with the woman who came down to the lobby to watch her son working across the road. He never asked why she didn't just run across and speak to him, as asking why had never fallen within his area of expertise. He wondered if his mother had ever watched him, and questioned if his own employment had been as coincidental as he had previously assumed.

Rick was seemingly unable to notice his son just across the street. He'd leave for work every morning, and his eyes would move over his son without really processing the figure in front of him.

The Doormen stood watching, occasionally catching a glimpse of the other letting people into their respective buildings. They were no longer interested in each other.

Through the Bracken and the Dirt

El Rose

For Percy, Evelyn, Charisma, and Tim. Thank you for giving me the space to breathe and be.

Whilst the house on the hill burnt, sparks playacting as stars in the night sky, Aled's mother cut the cord connecting them and kissed him on the top of his soft newborn head, mindless of the natural viscera adorning her beautiful son. She passed away moments later, alone in the storage shed she'd forced her way into, the story of her life extinguished save for her last living legacy still clutched to her cooling chest, waving around impossibly small fists. Aled was born with a cloak of stars cinched around his fragile neck, death's loving breath the first warmth to grace his cheek.

One life was born on the night three were lost to flame. One life saved by a fluke of fate.

If the manor had not burned, the shed would not have

been searched for buckets with which to carry more water to the blaze. If the shed had not been found, lock crudely broken, blood mistaken for rust on the handle, then Aled would have died and rotted with his only family. This was the first time death blessed Aled by parting freely and without debt.

Sometimes, looking back, Aled would wish death had not been so merciful.

He was found by one villager or the other, none would claim to be his saviour in the years to come and none, at the time, would harbour an ounce of familial affection for him. None could, or would, name the woman who had scraped her swollen feet raw to return to their small village in the dead of night. They had more important things to save. More familiar people to care and mourn for.

Later, much later, when Aled was a child full of words and innocent curiosity, he would ask the villagers how it was that no one could know who he belonged to. There were no children his age left in the valley and so he did not know how to play, he was not told or read stories of fantastical adventures upon which to model his life. He was alone in a forest of ageing people who wanted him only for the help he could provide. And still, Aled asked:

"Who was my mother?"

"No one knows," they would answer, softly the first time.

"Was she not there? When I was born?"

"No one knows who she was," they would answer the second time, if they bothered at all. "It does not matter, focus on the matter at hand", to the third as patience ran shallow with these people, they hadn't wanted to be where they were and they had no way out except for a child barely able to clean itself. "Be quiet or you'll be without dinner," they began to threaten after the fourth.

And yet Aled remained curious despite their silence.

"Did she not love me?"

"How did she die?"

"Who found me? Who named me?"

The answers became blunt. Then the only answer became a withdrawal of food. Then a hand across his cheek. A rod to his back. A night in the cellar. A post driven into the ground, fragile wrists tied together, blood mixing into mud under red-raw knees.

The only escape became silence. And from six years old onwards, Aled held his tongue so completely that the village believed him to have fallen mute, another dark mark to his name. Another excuse to continue without thought for human kindness. For mercy. For decency.

Not that he would ever know it, but it was a widower who took Aled in when he was born. In the midst of the chaos and the collective mourning of the village that tragic night, the valley's blacksmith lost his last vestige of hope for the natural goodness of the world. He had given up his wife to the family on the hill many years before and now he had lost his daughter to them as well. The others, his friends, his village, had hauled him down from the manor, physically dragging him through the bracken and the dirt of the path, burns fresh on his arms, his face, under his very nails. The village's square, solemnly silent aside from the trickling fountain holding vigil over them all, was full of the witnesses of the disaster. Some were dumbstruck, some were still weeping into their own fallen knees. Some, like him, burnt and soot stained, reeking of the smoke they'd plunged into to try to rescue someone, something, anything, were sitting on the lip of the stone fountain, being tended to by the elders of their community. The blacksmith was treated kindly. He was fed stale bread to help restore the steady cadence of his breath. Water was poured over his skin and he barely flinched. Consoling words were whispered in an unheard litany into his blistering hands.

He was a blacksmith by trade and a blacksmith by nature. Fire had always been his friend. His first love. His teacher. And now, after so long and deep a trust, he saw no way forward without swearing to turn his back on it. Never again would he light the fire of his forge. Never again would he trust the heat with his love. His life. And never, never again would he look upon magic with anything but distrust. He vowed this upon the resting peace of his wife and the memory of the body of his daughter seen and never to be forgotten.

Someone asked him what he saw there. Inside the manor. Inside his daughter's home.

Someone else answered for him, voice low, when he did not so much as close his eyes in reply. It was one of his neighbours; she had used her own coat to smother the flames that had clung desperately to his skin. He had broken her nose in the struggle, he had felt it crack under his knuckles.

"He will not speak," she said softly. "If that had been my daughter, I would have fought to stay there and die just as he did. We found him trying to put out the flames on her charred body with his own. He held onto her even as we pulled him out."

Another distant witness spoke up, voice shaking, "What happened to them? Who started it?"

"Her wife must have lost control at last. She was barely more than blood and bone next to Yarrow."

The blacksmith flinched, hard enough for the joint of his shoulder to pop like the flames now so far away. His caretakers presumed it a reaction to the cold and wrapped a well-loved blanket around him, the corners of it falling carelessly into the fountain's depths. They patted him on the back and turned away, returning to their conversation. He cast about for something else to focus on.

The fire was still raging, a bright spot casting the rest of the hillside in impenetrable darkness. He couldn't look away now he'd met its glare. A perilous vindication itched under his blistering skin, entwined and yet also sharply separate from his grief. He didn't even know what had happened. He didn't know whether it was his daughter's wife, a woman so loyal and kind-hearted that he wasn't even sure how to think ill of her in death. Yarrow should have been safe with her. Should have been safe in her own home.

There was no way for him to know how long it was before the second call of the night arose from somewhere behind him, toward the other side of the valley. People rushed away to help, to control the newest disaster. A community in focus. The bonds of hard won lives put into practice. They returned quickly, with unexpectedly recognisable cries coming with the arms of a man with blood on his hands and forehead. At last the blacksmith turned away from his daughter's pyre. A babe. Just born. Sickly in colour and naked to the chill of the night.

The rescuer passed the child away to the person next to him before scrubbing off the crimson from his hands into the fountain, adding more clouds of dirt and grime to the already sullied waters. It was with a distant sense of disdain that the blacksmith watched the villagers pass up the child, each denying a connection to the poor soul, each refusing to take him into their arms again. They did not wrap the vulnerable child in a blanket as they had wrapped him. They did not wash off the baby's blood. They did not handle him gently, resulting in shakey squawks of protest, panicked confusion, whining forth from the smallest chest he'd ever seen. Yarrow had never been so small. But this child was. And this child needed care. He could give that. He could do that. Right now, when his world was still flaking into ash, when everything felt impossible and unnecessary, this he could do.

With a tight band around his lungs and a visible shake, he cracked to his aching feet, dragging the blanket over his shoulder, tugging off his shirt, and, with a sharp look pointed at the woman currently smothering the child's cries with her hand, took the babe into his own arms. The blacksmith cleaned the grime and evidence of the boy's birth with the remnants of his shirt before wrapping him securely in the blanket, mindful of its damp edges, and cradling the child to his bare chest. Death smiled to see the babe taken out of his path once more.

He kept Aled close to his heart for the next two years.

~

Magic for Aled was like the sun on his skin. The air in his lungs. The balls of the joints of his knees. It was easy. It was simple. It was uncontainable. Hooked deep into his skin, a noose around his neck. What would have brought a normal witch to blindness or the loss of a limb left only a momentary twinge at the top of his spine. He was a power incarnate. A cracked vessel leaking magic and yet holding it in his every atom. The blacksmith knew this within weeks of taking Aled in and he did not tell a soul. His wife had been the village witch. Long after her death he, as the all the others, had held onto the expectation that his daughter would be the next to show an aptitude for the impossible but it fell to one of the twins on the hill. The manor girl became his daughter's wife. And, as far as anyone believed, her cause of death. And so he knew as much about it as one could without the scars could. Intimately, he knew the costs and the risks. And so he knew that Aled was an anomaly.

Every day something was broken by Aled's infant waves of uncoordinated magic and what could not be repaired by the blacksmith himself or thrown into the cottage's fireplace had to be stored in the coal shed behind the house; he could not risk the others of the village becoming more suspicious. He kept the windows closed, the curtains drawn, to avoid peering eyes and trusted that the others would attribute it to mourning if they cared to notice at all.

Each person in the village had come to the blacksmith's door with messages of help and hope and often bowls of food. He answered them kindly, returning their dishes clean and empty. Within months the well-wishes became polite enquiries as to when he was returning to work. Then they became pleas. Then demands.

The harvest was rotting in the fields, they said, we need new tools.

Our family heard something in the trees, at least sharpen our swords, they begged.

We are without a witch, without a healer, can you truly expect us to also be without a blacksmith? What trade can we do now? You are cursing us all to starve! Have you no care for your people?

To each and every one the blacksmith said no. He could not. He would not. What he had made for them before was strong and built to last, he knew his work and knew his skill, they did not truly need his hands in the flames of the forge. His role was as father now, nothing more and nothing less. The results of his labour were the smiles Aled gifted him so freely, the calmness of the house after hours of lullabies was now his most used trick. So he continued to turn them down.

The simultaneous loss of witch, healer, and blacksmith left the people of the valley largely unemployed and without means of transport or trade. With unemployment came poverty and with poverty came fallout. More and more they turned away visitors to their valley. Less and less they left to trade elsewhere as they had nothing spare to trade. They had been without a village witch before but never had they lost two witches so close together. As far as everyone but the blacksmith was aware, it was at least a thirteen year wait until the next witch would come into their gifts, if they had been born the year of Marian's death at all. Sometimes they came later. Without the power being sunk into the earth, the fields struggled to nurture the crops they planted. Without experienced hands to cure and heal, illness ran rampant through the community when brought in from outside their streets. Without trust, people became desperate, became cold, became selfish.

Many of his old neighbours and friends refused to speak to him until he returned to work. But he had Aled, he was not alone nor lonely. Still, the looks were becoming worse and it was not until he'd reached the washing river, Aled wrapped safe and asleep on his back, that he heard just how far the village's resentment had grown.

Anora lost her child, just this morning. He was playing

by the well, fell over the edge. No one knew for hours that he'd even been awake let alone out the house at such a time.

Aye, he's to be buried next to Wilson's little one. To think, the two of them not even five years old. There's a blight on the land since the burning.

If the blacksmith would leave that child be these things wouldn't be happening. Anora wouldn't have been in the fields and Tommy Wilson wouldn't have been so exhausted as he was.

Should've left it with the mother. No need to bring it in like he did. We can't be affording to feed another mouth.

There hasn't been a single birth since, Anora's was the last. Then the fire child, what's it's name? And nothing since. Not a one. Something's wrong here.

Bad luck, that babe. Should be-

The blacksmith turned upriver before he could hear the rest.

Aled's growth was the spark they'd need to do exactly as they wished. He couldn't keep Aled hidden forever, he knew that. He was familiar, now, with death's gaze on the back of his neck.

The blacksmith did not wish to sleep most nights, wary of the paths his dreams would tread, and so Aled's constant needs and daytime isolation were an excuse he gladly latched onto, taking the child outside in the only hours he deemed it safe, when the moon was high and they could wander without light to the edge of the village trails and stare up the walls of the valley hills. Here, in these indistinct hours, feeling safer and more free than he ever did during the day, the blacksmith told stories of his daughter to his unexpected son. Aled, wide grey eyes blinking slowly, would listen often without complaint, calmed by the rumble of the blacksmith's voice. The villagers would grumble whenever Aled cried and squawled and screamed on their nightly walks, but none wanted to offer aid to the child so none came out and saw something they shouldn't.

Death came quick and painless for every child in the valley but Aled that first year of the aftermath. The blacksmith lay flowers on the new graves every full moon when the light was enough to read the rough engravings and whisper prayers to the clear skies, Aled sitting up on his own in the damp grass.

With walking and independent thought came more incidents. More cracks in the windows. More plants in the garden blossoming out of season whilst the rest of the valley wilted. More mad, hiccuping giggles that threw rainbows scattering brightly, impossibly through their house. More screams that killed the sparrows nesting on their roof. More and more and more magic that was harder and harder to explain away and yet no cuts, no bruises, no marks to strike the natural balance upon his little body. The blacksmith tried his best but he was not a fool and when poorly muffled footsteps followed him one nightly walk with a dozing Aled in his arms, he knew their time was up. Death walked beside him at the last, comforting in inevitability.

The blacksmith took the dirt path up the hill, overgrown and still scarred from the horror, nothing had grown. Nothing had healed. Aled was none the wiser, blissfully ignorant to Death's whispers through the night around him. The blacksmith's followers were not clever, they were not even particularly strong, not compared to his years of heavy work. But they were desperate. And to them what he carried was not an innocent child, but a tool, a way out of it all. They had finally put together the pieces of the puzzle and Aled was no longer a burden but now a freak of nature they could chain up for their own needs. And so they would.

The blacksmith never made it to the skeleton of the manor on his own. The last courtesy the village people did him was to throw his body in the heap that they presumed his daughter and daughter in law to have burned in. Death took him gently and watched Aled be carried away with regret in her heart.

Aled would, whilst climbing the fragile ribs remaining of the manor, bury the blacksmith when he dislodged a supporting beam and crumbled the last of the entry hall wall down by accident, trying to feel the breeze in his hair when he was fifteen and desperate not to be found.

~

Gwydion arrived to less fanfare than he was used to.

Being the only travelling village witch, as far as he'd ever heard, was something unique and, typically, warmly celebrated by those he deigned to lend his help to. It was, after all, expected for witches to stay home in the communities that birthed them; stationary and, as far as Gwydion was concerned, stagnant. At the tender age of sixteen, three years into his training with the brother of the deceased witch who came before him, he packed up, fashioned a walking stick as he passed the final farmhouse, and turned his back forever.

He'd never so much as glanced over his shoulder, never feeling the need. He had everything he could ever want in the bag on his back and anything he didn't have he could conjure with a bit of thought and maybe a couple vials worth of blood. Perhaps a puddle's worth if he wanted something particularly large. The wind in his hair, untangling his tight braids with tricksy fingers, and the sun gilding his skin was all he needed to carry him through life. His name, his manner of trade, and his wilfulness to help where the money was good, spread as rumour and gossip into stories of renown as he crossed the mountains and valleys of their great lonely land. Gwydion kept his past a mystery, mastering the party tricks of evasive answers and distracting touches in the pub or the market square or the occasional hay barn. He was exactly who he had wanted to become when he first left home with dreams in his head and a handful of scars upon his skin. He did not fear Death and danger was a partner he loved to dance with.

Now, at a wise twenty-five years old, Gwydion was consciously moving into more of a proud stride as the village he'd heard so much about came into view. Squat blue and grey cottages dappled like patches of sunlight in the fields, connected by time worn roads. Nothing exceptional. What looked to be a square for market stalls and visiting caravans somewhat centrally situated within the clusters of homes, a pretty but neglected round fountain in the middle. The fields he was passing by, and occasionally carving a sneaky path through, were flourishing to a degree he'd never seen before in his life. Corn the size of his arm, stalks thicker than he could push past. The most vibrant shades of green from border bush to border bush, glimmering pleasantly as if caught forever in the sun's rays even when the sky itself was clouded over. Unnervingly pristine and clearly the work of the local witch. And clearly, to Gwydion, of a calibre of power that would take him weeks to recover from expelling into such large swathes of earth. But was this not the reason he'd made the journey? Was this not the whole point of coming to this middle-of-nowhere hamlet, he reminded himself, whoever was doing such monumental work was at least worth knowing, if not learning from, surely?

And with a witch so powerful as their own, rooted as deep into the land as their overarching orchard to the south of the square suggested they must be, it wasn't that much of a surprise that there was no welcome party. No. He couldn't expect to be lauded here. But that was fine, he thought as he yanked his cloak out of the grasp of a particularly enterprising blackberry bush, perfectly fine. A new experience! How refreshing. The torn threads of his clothes were less refreshing but he would fix them up later, should he have any energy left after seeing to whatever the local witch might request his help with or hadn't gotten around to that day.

Still, even with expectations sufficiently lowered, Gwydion was rather disappointed by the utter lack of anyone upon stepping foot into the square. He'd been through his fair share of poverty stricken villages, he knew the signs of a community hiding in their homes from the threat of a plague or saving what precious energy they had by remaining in bed during a famine. There were none of the usual signs here. Everything but the fountain was in good condition. The weather was pleasant. The air clear of smoke. He spun in a bemused circle, heels of his boots clicking against the cobble ground. Well. Better to wait to be found than to impose himself upon the populace.

Gwydion set his pack down to lean against the fountain and decided to take a walk around the square's edges, taking in the admittedly rather majestic views of the valley's forested sides. There seemed to be a blacksmith's forge and shop set next to a couple of cottages down one of the numerous tracks branching away from the paved square. A bakery, with incredibly clear windows showing off an array of loaves and cakes, down another. What might have been a small rudimentary school but also could have been a village hall up a slight incline. Down towards the orchard was a large, well-kept field with the occasional festive ribbon sun-bleached but still tightly tied to branches of the trees dotting the country dancing space. Gwydion turned to the hill he'd come down, marvelling at his own progress, before turning to the view opposite. Taller, this one, but with more levelled-off shelves, some big enough to potentially build upon. A particularly high one that looked to be pretty sturdy just there up to the- Gwydion squinted against the sun and flicked his gaze back to a suspicious dark spot he'd passed over before on first look. He hummed, a low inquisitive sound he knew he was prone to making without realising because he'd thought it a fun quirk to be known for when he was nineteen, and took a step off of the cobbles to get a better look. No sooner had he shielded his eyes from the glaring light, feet planted in the dry dirt, did he hear a short scream from somewhere to his right.

Wheeling around on his heel, Gwydion searched for the cause of the noise. Nothing.

He waited.
Listened.
Looked.
A shout. A called name.
There.

In one of the fields, a group of people, indistinct. Moving intermittently. Nothing alarming, more than likely a scream of joy then. Celebrating something else perfect in this perfect place.

With a renewed sense of purpose, Gwydion grabbed his bag and, without a care for the time it took, meandered down the path to the little gathering.

There seemed to be quite a few of them. Men and women. No children. The closer he got, the more he could hear. He strained to make out more, to understand more, until there was a crack in the air. A ripple of lightning through a stormcloud, static and sharp like a whip making contact. Gwydion's breath escaped his lungs like he'd been punched in the stomach, shoulders hunching, bag hitting the ground with a careless thump. But he hadn't been the one hit. One of the men had hit someone else in the crowd, a slight figure who took the blow without giving a single sign as to how much the world around them had reacted to his injury. None of the people gathered seemed to notice the shockwave that had so nearly flattened Gwydion with its force. They hadn't felt it. The victim had to be the witch and he had to have displaced his pain to the threads of magic he'd flushed this place with, he was entwined with the very air. Gwydion had never even heard of such a thing being possible. And yet here they were. Gwydion winded and wincing from the magical reverberation and the witch himself utterly still.

The man who had hit the witch turned his back on him, shaking his hand out. No one else seemed to care, they were crouching down around someone else. Had the man, the one who got hit, the witch, had he done something to hurt someone? Gwydion had seen only one witch abuse their power. He had sworn never to be the same. He had also left Death to finish the job he'd been hired for.

A woman sobbed, her cries rushing to fill the empty air after the witch's magic had snapped up what felt like all the natural sounds of the summer day. Gwydion, forgetting his bag and his grand entrance, took off at a sprint, vaulting the gate into what turned out to be a pumpkin field with an entirely out of season bounty of fruit. He landed perfectly on his feet, drawing the attention immediately of everyone there.

He'd been right that the majority were kneeling around someone else, the weeping woman it seemed, though they now closed ranks defensively around her. Stood to the side, a cold distance away, was the witch. Gwydion looked him over once, already not liking his impassive stance and when it was clear, which was within one second of Gwydion's attention, that he wasn't going to try to continue helping if in fact he had even been helping before, Gwydion turned away. He raised his hands carefully, his loose sleeves falling away to show off the scars on his forearms, the half a pinky-finger that he had on his left hand.

"You're a witch?" It was one of the women, grey-haired, shoulder to shoulder with one of the youngest of the lads hiding their fallen friend.

Gwydion nodded, lowering his hands. "Yes. I am. Do you need help?"

He'd expected the suspicious exchange of glances between them all. He was almost always met with caution when he first arrived. A wandering witch surely had no reason to be wandering if they were any good at either their job or at being a moral person. But the truth was, he was good. At both. And people in need tended not to be able to afford to not trust him, at least to begin with.

"You got any experience with childbirth?" The voice this time came from down near the floor, somewhere behind the defensive wall.

Gwydion kept his expression serene, composed,

helpful. "Sure, is someone giving birth?" And, because he couldn't help but be curious about the strange witch at his back, "Is your witch away? Tad inconvenient timing, that, isn't it."

None of them so much as softened at his attempt at humour. In fact, they all seemed to tense, even the crying woman, apparently with child, hushed up. Each gaze slid over his shoulder. Gwydion, slightly unnerved, reluctantly joined them in their collective viewing, somewhat hysterically thinking there'd be some beast of a man with a rather large knife or something else absurd standing where the witch had been. There wasn't. Of course there wasn't.

It was just the witch. Head down, short dark hair just about hiding his face from view. Shoulders in a tense straight line. His whole stick-thin body held to the most absolute level of statuesque stillness. It barely looked like he was breathing. Though that wasn't helped by his incredibly ill-fitting clothes, hanging loose like old rags on a scarecrow. The witch didn't look up. Didn't register their attention other than to move his arms behind his back, giving Gwydion only a flash of long, characteristically thin fingers. Well. Fine. If that was how it was going to be, so be it.

Gwydion turned back to the villagers and tried to convey that he could be trusted with... delicate situations with only a small smile and a nod. "May I take a look?"

Another beat of hesitation but they did acquiesce. Shifting to the side to let him through.

He knew from the start that it was a waste of energy to try anything magical at all. The woman was kneeling in a veritable bog of blood and grass and sweat. Miscarriage. She looked barely to have even had a bump yet. A shame. A tragedy. A trauma. But not unusual. Not something he could remedy with any amount of focus, work, or determination. Not even bleeding himself into a coma could bring back what had been lost here.

Still...

Still, he knelt down, flicking away the thought that his trousers would get dirty, and took the woman's hands in his own, gentle. She looked up at him, crestfallen.

"Are you still bleeding," Gwydion asked softly. She mutely shook her head. "Did something happen?" He thought back to the witch getting hit, the blanching of the universe that none of them had felt, he wondered which of these men standing above him had done it.

Again, she shook her head. "This is just how it is here," she said, a dry tone of resignation to her words. "There hasn't been a child here since the burning. We just...we hoped still, you know? We keep hoping."

Gwydion nodded, not quite understanding but more than willing to lie to ease her agony. "Are you in pain? Any pain at all?"

"No. No, it never hurts."

"This is her third." Gwydion looked up into the face of the elder woman from before. "We haven't had a child here for years."

Gwydion nodded, careful not to let his confusion show. "Right. Has your witch done the usual checks? The water, the soil? Checked for a disease?"

Again, the look up to the witch that none of them had yet vocally claimed as their witch. Gwydion, again, followed their gaze. The flinch upon meeting the man's eyes now he was on the ground was unavoidable, unquenchable. Seeming either not to care or not to notice, somehow, the witch nodded.

"Yes," one of the people said aloud, seemingly speaking for the witch, but Gwydion couldn't tear his gaze away from those damn stone-cold eyes yet, not now he sort of had their attention, "he has. He hasn't found anything useful and continues to do nothing else to help us."

From down on the ground, the witch's hair didn't hide him the way it had before and Gwydion noticed the flicker of disagreement flash across his sharp features. He noticed and determined to have a word with the man after he had ensured everything was back to normal for these people.

It didn't take long to be allowed to get them moving. On the walk back to the woman's home, her husband, the one Gwydion was now quite confident had attacked the witch, supported her every step along the way. It wasn't a long walk by any means but it was enough for Gwydion to give a quick rundown of who he was and what he did. When he offered to help out with anything their witch had yet to or hadn't been able to do, there was an odd shared look on everyone's faces as they thanked him. Not that they offered him any work. Well, he thought, maybe this witch is good at organising or something, inability to help with fertility aside.

The villagers left him without telling him of anywhere he could stay which was less than ideal but it looked to be a peaceful night and he was no stranger to sleeping rough. The summer days were long and the nights short enough not to freeze a soul stretched out under the stars. So, left to his own devices, Gwydion started to trace his steps backwards in the hopes of finding his forgotten bag.

He'd just checked around the fountain when a hand shoved its abrupt way into his face, bag straps looking far too heavy for such thin fingers. Gwydion straightened and came face to almost face with the witch. Still holding out his bag. Gwydion raised an eyebrow at the complete lack of greeting or manners but when no words at all seemed forthcoming, took his proffered belongings.

"I don't think we actually introduced ourselves, before I mean," Gwydion started for them, at least trying to get off on a civil footing.

Nothing.

"In the field," he tried again, "with the blood and all?"

Not a single noticeable change. Gwydion nodded, more to himself than the other man.

"Well, my name is Gwydion. I come from here, there and everywhere and if you don't mind another witch about, I figured I would stick around to try and help you fix this whole child problem you seem to be having, seeing as you seem to be a touch stuck with it. What say you?"

Gwydion was, and would forever after be, ashamed that he'd only tacked on the question at the end to taunt the man. He would in fact flush an alarming shade of red and wish aloud to throw himself in the nearest river when he learned that the first words he heard from the witch were in fact the first words the witch had spoken since he was but a very, very young child.

"Do you need somewhere to stay?"

Well. Way to make him look like an arsehole, Gwydion thought. Not that that stopped him from digging himself an even deeper hole, as was his way.

"Not sure I want to stay with a man who doesn't even tell his name. Doesn't seem the smartest thing for a wandering singleton like myself to do now, does it? Who knows what you do in your spare time. You could murder lambs for fun for all I know. Maybe that's the whole thing behind-"

Gwydion was incredibly grateful when the man cut him off mid-sentence.

"Aled."

"Excuse me?" Gwydion said without coherent intention.

The man- the witch- Aled, tensed up even more. Which Gwydion hadn't thought was possible. He waited to see if Aled would repeat himself or look at him or quite frankly do anything at all, but it didn't seem to be happening. Literal crickets chirped.

Gwydion stuck a hand out, the left one. "Nice to meet you, Aled."

If it wasn't so likely that it was just his imagination, Gwydion could have sworn that Aled smiled. Just a little.

Aled took his hand with a soft shake, like he wasn't really sure what he was doing. There was a spark that was most definitely not Gwydion's imagination as they came into contact, how much damned magic did this man have? To be shooting off sparks like it was normal and- Wait-

Gwydion turned his grip into a vice, pulling an unsuspecting Aled a couple of steps closer as he pushed up the man's oversized shirt sleeve. Gwydion twisted Aled's arm this way and that, then, when Aled gave a tug to pull away, Gwydion ducked, without letting go, to see past Aled's hair, bypassing those stormcloud eyes to check elsewhere.

"What the hell are you?" Gwydion breathed aloud; Aled tugged again, those pinprick sparks snapping up again, visibly white hot and yet painless this time. "Have you done any damned magic in your entire life? Did you at fucking all try to help that woman and her child? Have you ever? The last witch must have died a week ago for the place to be like it is still! How much have you inherited? And you're not using it to help them? What fucking excuse do you possibly have?"

It was with a surprising amount of strength for such a bird-boned body that Aled yanked himself away, straightening up to a height that Gwydion hadn't quite expected. Aled was looking at him for sure now, brow furrowed and lips downturned in irritation.

"I helped." Aled's voice was cold, blank as slate. Gwydion had never heard a voice so rough, like the scrape of bark catching against his coat, harsh. "There was nothing else anyone could do. Is nothing."

Gwydion shook his head in disbelief. Not a single scar on the man. Not a cut or graze, not a single instance of bodily harm to mark the cost he paid for the power he used. Incredible. Abysmal.

"I'll see about that. Using some god damned magic might help for a start," Gwydion snapped.

"Nothing you do will be any different."

No. Gwydion was done with this.

He slung his bag over his shoulder and set off for the festival field, planning to set up camp under one of the willow trees. His blood was boiling in his veins, furious at the witch's indifference. He hadn't even defended himself properly. It was sick. To have so much power as he so clearly did and not to use it.

Aled didn't call out after him. Didn't follow him.

Gwydion shoved aside the plummeting rock in his chest as nothing more than the disappointment it was.

~

It had been a week since Gwydion's arrival and the village was becoming too comfortable around the wandering witch. The man was a wanderer and wander he did. They weren't Aled's secrets to keep but they would be his punishments to be had if they had to explain things to their visitor.

Aled was still in constant demand. In the fields, at the wells, to try to fumble his way through forging things as no new blacksmith had ever moved into the old cottage. His fellow people hadn't bothered to try to get him to speak since he was twelve but Gwydion hadn't been quiet about telling them all of their conversation. The villagers didn't believe him, leaving Gwydion to awkwardly laugh as if he'd intended to make a joke. In fact, it seemed to Aled that Gwydion was never quiet. Forever talking, laughing, offering to help with absolutely anything. Sometimes watching Aled from afar with uncompromising eyes even as Gwydion seemed otherwise utterly engaged in telling a story of his travels.

Aled hated him.

Aled was fascinated by him.

Here was a man, a witch no less, flying on wings of the purest forms of freedom. He went where he wanted. Did as he pleased. Charmed everyone he met. He had a purpose he had chosen and the means to pursue it wherever it took him, and the scars to prove he did it well. He did not have to climb the ruins of a manor to feel even a hint of imagined peace.

Aled had none of that.

The burns and hits from the villagers would be healed in seconds by the force inside him, before he even realised he'd been hurt sometimes. A whirlwind he still couldn't really control lived in the gaps between his ribs and the space inside his lungs and the beat of his heart and it was both the destruction and the entirety of his life. The only thing they had ever found to last for longer than a blink was the unrelenting cracks of the whips, especially the ones they no longer had horses to use with, killed when Aled couldn't heal their crippled legs. Each time was just as torturous as the first. The damage too deep and inflicted too fast for his magic to bypass the shock and heal with any sort of efficiency. Still, it happened a lot less now. They had broken him young. The post still stood, the ropes still swayed in the wind, behind the beehives in the orchard, out of the way. Gwydion hadn't been shown that on his tour.

Magic for Aled was a curse. A clock ticking down to the moment he did more than accidentally break a window or kill off a herd of cows. That particular incident was one the villagers had brought upon themselves, not that Aled had received any sort of reprieve afterwards. They'd simply started holding back the whip when in the fields, had relocated the post to its current home. He had been thirteen.

It was with only a pretence of surprise that Aled turned to face Gwydion one evening by the fountain. He had been watching him all day and Aled knew why. Of course he knew why. The magic had been gnawing inside of him, biting and clawing and scraping its way out of him with more and more desperation since Gwydion had shaken his hand. He had to let it out. If he did not let it out, the next time he went to the post it would be like he was thirteen all over again and the closest thing for his power to immolate this time wouldn't be cows.

Gwydion, as had proved usual, didn't hold up with any niceties for Aled.

"What are you doing?"

Aled didn't know why he kept answering. He didn't know why he wanted to. He did not know why, now, he did not lie.

"Offloading."

Gwydion frowned, his eyes always narrowed when he frowned. Aled could feel it, in the same way he felt everything in the valley from the ladybird in the grass to the rolling of the clouds above them to the breaths of every person in their homes. Aled's home was one damp room at the slope of the hill, the skeleton of the old manor house looming above him every time he stepped outside his door. His land, though, his land stretched up and down the entire valley.

"Not cryptic at all. Nor suspicious."

"You think everything I do is suspicious," Aled reminded him flatly, turning back to sit on the fountain's edge, fingertips trailing into the water.

"Have you considered that perhaps you simply are suspicious? Or at least, mysterious in a not so welcoming way?"

Aled nodded, focusing inwards, ignoring those watching eyes, letting the magic keening inside him stretch outwards. Little by little. Tugging it back when it tried to race up the inside of a timber frame or curl up in Gwydion's trouser pocket too fast. Utmost attention. Absolute control. To keep it in completely led to accidents. To let it out entirely would end in destruction. So it was bit by bit. With the sun setting and the valley darkening, everyone else eating dinner, leaving him be for a precious slip of time. Here and now he could embrace the world he was part of. The world he was.

~

"What are you doing?" Gwydion heard himself repeating, barely registering that he'd spoken, definitely not expecting an answer as Aled's back curved in and in and in over the water.

There was a heat crawling up his skin. Radiating out from the smooth-skinned witch sitting before him. Metaphysical. Magical. Warm nearly to the point of discomfort. Digging deep under his skin, humming in the thin layer between cloth and body, lighting up every drop of magical energy in Gwydion. It all came back to that one question. The one nobody in this village would answer. The one Gwydion was beginning to think he would not like the answer to.

"What are you?"

Aled looked up at him and his grey eyes were white. Entirely white. The white of heated metal. Of burning charcoal. Of the full moon on a clear night. Their eyes met and then Aled shuddered, eyes snapping shut, body closing in on itself. And all at once the heat vanished and Gwydion was suddenly freezing, the abrupt change dropping him to his knees, like whatever Aled had been doing had been the only thing holding him up. Aled ducked his face away, leaning back over the water behind him, fingers curling over his knees.

They said nothing.

"I'm sorry," Aled said, hushed, at last.

Gwydion's answering laugh was harsh, a scraped out sort of sound. Things weren't adding up neatly anymore. The churning of his stomach suggested that it never had.

"Do some magic for me? Anything strong, anything that requires a bit of focus," Gwydion asked, ready to test a new theory. Ready to do more than watch and wait.

Aled was still for so long that Gwydion began to think he wasn't going to do as asked, but then, there in Gwydion's lap, grew a scattering of light, like sparks from a fire, glowing and fading. The cluster grew and grew until Gwydion started to pick out familiar shapes from the chaos.

They were stars. Aled was conjuring a perfect miniature projection of the night sky. Just like that.

Gwydion took his time to watch for a twitching muscle, a drop of crimson, a cramping toe and when none came he whistled appreciatively and the stars disappeared in a blink. "You know," he started, softly, carefully, "I'd have been bleeding from under my fingernails to make even half of that."

Aled looked up, visibly startled as he looked to check whether Gwydion's fingernails were bleeding. They weren't. Had he ever bled, Gwydion wondered, had he ever known pain?

"So," Gwydion continued, "please believe me when I say I am sorry for accusing you baselessly. It is clear from the sheer natural life of this place, that a strong witch indeed has been caring for it. I was wrong to dismiss your attempts to help your people as I did."

"You can't help them."

Gwydion shook his head. "No. I cannot. You did everything you could to help that woman. To help all these people with their children. I am sorry to have suggested otherwise."

Aled's fingers clenched into fists and he stood in one solid movement. Graceful but perfunctory. "Thank you for trying."

Gwydion, still on his knees on the cobbles, reached out without really thinking it through, resting a hand over one of Aled's trembling fists. Aled's eyes were flecked with that eerie white, like snow from heavy clouds.

"Why did he hit you? That first day?"

Aled flinched. Hard. But he didn't pull away from Gwydion's touch.

"Ask them. Any of them. Not me."

~

There was a time, in Gwydion's past, when blood had not slid from between the sides of gashes in the skin of his legs. He did not always have the scar that had nearly cost him his life, a great valley of his own down his back from the base of his neck to the last of the divots of spine, sometimes deep and sometimes shallow. Always mottled and tough to the touch. The greatest cost he'd ever paid for the greatest gift he'd ever taken for himself without permission. Eventually one of Aled's villagers asked him why he walked. Why he travelled. They always asked. He always lied.

This time, with Aled's flinch in his mind's eye, he told the truth. A secret for an honest answer and the villager, the young woman he couldn't help that first day, agreed immediately, curiosity lighting up her worn face. So he told her about the need to run, the desperation to carve his own path and escape the suffocating nothingness of the village. He showed her the top of his scar, let her run her fingertips over it and swallowed down the disgust at her touch, recounted how he'd ripped the memories of his existence from his entire village and in doing so nearly ripped himself in half. Her husband watched him carefully from the fireplace. He smiled at him soothingly.

And, satisfied, she prompted him to ask his question.

He kept his eyes on the husband.

"How often have you hurt Aled?"

This time round, the tour included an out of the way post behind a flourishing collection of beehives in an unerringly perfect orchard in a village haunted by the smallest of graves.

~

Aled spent the next day waiting for the worst. So when the worst came, it was a lot less angry at him than Aled had expected. Not to say that Gwydion wasn't angry. He without a doubt was furious and his muttering wasn't quiet. But he wasn't the strongest of the villagers coming to tie him to the post. He wasn't trying to curse Aled to choke on his own tongue, yet at least. Gwydion found Aled waiting outside the shack he called home. Striding down the path, pack on his back, and a stoney expression on his lively face. Aled ducked his head and was ready to let the tirade wash over him as best he could let it. It was, after all, his fault. He was the one to have cursed them all. His birth started it all. Death had tied itself to him and it was his shadow that Death herself lingered in.

"Aled!"

He was the angry child who let go of control. Who couldn't reforge the horse's cartilage.

"Aled, you had better listen to me."

He was the full-grown adult who still couldn't clean up his mess. Who still hadn't done enough, been enough, repented enough to earn a reprieve from punishment.

"Hey."

A hand slipped into view between him and the grass at his feet. Scarred and bruised fingers. Belonging to a man who wasn't... who was...

The gentlest of hesitant touches to his cheek, thumb tracing his cheekbone. Touch. He hadn't- Had he ever- Was this-

"Aled. Listen to me, please. Listen."

"You..."

That wandering thumb pressed against his lips and he flushed, trying to focus on Gwydion's shoes instead. Bracing for the change into violence. Of course. Yes. He had been touched like this before. But he hadn't been hurt by another witch before. Maybe it would be like the whip. Or maybe not. Maybe it could be even worse. A mix of them all. New.

Gwydion's breath heaved out of him.

"I'm not- I'm so sorry, Aled. What they've done- I can't- I just can't. Aled. Come with me. I'm begging you. This isn't right. This isn't the world and it is not the only way to live. It isn't any way to live."

Aled shook his head, pulling back, and tilted his head up to look Gwydion in the eye. Gwydion didn't know what he was talking about and whilst he wasn't going to ask for it, he couldn't linger in Gwydion's touch, it was always a trap. Always. "I-"

"No!" Gwydion winced, lowered his voice. "Sorry, but no, Aled. I cannot let this go on, cannot leave you here alone. You- you've been so alone, my friend."

He bit his lip, hard. This wasn't right. This was not how it was meant to go. He was not this man's friend and he was not going to take his curse elsewhere. He was leashed to Death and her to him and to leave would be to take her elsewhere, to bring others into her path.

"Aled, stop, stop, please. You're not- what are you talking about? Death isn't- good god what have they been telling you, Aled?"

Aled took a step back and tried not to let his chest cave

in like it wanted when Gwydion followed him, causing Gwydion to look incredibly consternated which felt like it could be humorous any other time. "What did they tell you?"

Gwydion's expression hardened again and there, again there, a hand on his. "The truth. I don't appreciate being lied to so I made them tell me the truth. All of it." And, as if to prove it, he lifted Aled's hand to press against Gwydion's side, under his coat but over his shirt. His ribs could barely be felt, Aled marvelled, feeling ridiculous until his hand came away red and slick.

"Oh." Oh. Oh.

"Please. Don't see it as me helping you, I won't force you, I can't force you. But I will ask, I am asking, Aled."

"Asking..."

"Yes. I- You. Help yourself," Gwydion was practically stuttering, cutting himself off so often and Aled didn't know where the man's confidence had gone, he'd thought Gwydion to be all confidence, nothing to confuse or knock him off his course. "I am asking you to help yourself. Which," Gwydion took a steadying breath and he was still holding Aled's hand and Aled still wanted to answer, "really, is me asking you to leave with me. You don't have to stay with me, not to say I wouldn't like you to, but that- It isn't important-"

Aled cut in, starting to hope and he'd never felt that before and he was, frankly, terrified. "They would never let me."

Gwydion's will resolved itself before Aled's eyes, still and serious and watching, always watching. "They cannot stop you."

Aled took a breath. Took another. Cleared away the fear, the memories, the threats. He stepped in close to Gwydion, pushing up his shirt, all the while distancing himself from his own body, even as he healed Gwydion from the inside out. Even when Gwydion gripped his elbows and pressed their foreheads together as if he just knew that he needed to be grounded lest he slip away entirely. Aled drifted further out, searching, identifying. He let the heat spread. Finding where they all were. The sparks skittering around him were surely stinging Gwydion but the man was radiating danger himself, his blood drying on Aled's fingers still, crusting under his nails. He smelt of death.

"Leave them behind, Aled. Stop them from following." Gwydion's breath was nothing on his cheek, mere vibrations in his ear. His words were a match in the coal mine.

Aled let it go. Not everything. He was not cruel, still, after all their neglect and abuse, he was still not cruel. His eyes burnt white.

~

Whilst the village burnt, Gwydion pulled Aled's head down and pressed a kiss to his hair, a gleeful smile splitting his face.

"You are nothing I have ever seen before," Gwydion said, fiercely, kissing him again.

Aled took it as the first compliment he had ever received, tasting his first bite of freedom whilst encircled in Death's adoring arms.

About the Authors - 2022

2nd edition

Alastair Raper is an author from England, now living in Donegal, Ireland. He enjoys writing short horror, having contributed to stories to three other anthologies of dark fiction, including the two previous parts of the 'Roots' series. Through a love of telling tales of darkness and horror that he discovered while contributing to these anthologies, Alastair has also begun to write monthly horror stories on his Patreon site, 'Alastair's Writing World'. Through writing short stories, he finds a constant stream of fresh ideas that are beneficial for his other, longer-term projects, which include novels in both the Fantasy and Science Fiction genres.

James Morfa is a writer, poet and film maker who grew up in the Merseyside hinterlands but now spends most of his time in North Wales. His writing indulges in the strange, the surreal and the excessively queer, and he takes his inspirations from pretty much anywhere in literature between 1890 and 1939, as well as from classical and Norse mythology. He is also inadvertently responsible for Bangor University Writer's Guild's No. #1 character ship.

Imogen Morgan is an English Literature student at the University of Sheffield. She primarily enjoys writing about things that are unsettling, whether in her poetry or prose. She has written and narrated short stories for a horror audio-drama project, which can be found on YouTube at @talesfromthetwistedmind. She has previously been published in her university's creative writing journal, Route 57. When she isn't writing down her newest story idea, she can usually be found listening to her favourite horror audio dramas, where she gets most of her inspiration. Imogen can be contacted via email -
imogengracemorgan@gmail.co.uk -
or on Instagram under the username @kvothees where she occasionally posts her work.

Ben Fitzsimons is a writer who usually focuses on comedy (except for in this story which is not funny at all). As this is the only story he has successfully had published after his creative writing degree from Bangor University, he's now having a crisis of faith and considering exclusively writing vaguely creepy stories about apartment buildings in the pursuit of fame and glory.

El Rose is an author of all things fantastically queer. She uses her stories and poetry to give voice to neurodivergent worlds and queer lives. Her first solo publication, The Fisherman, is an experimental exploration of autistic perception and memory, also published with Barnard Publishing. The short story in this anthology, 'Through The Bracken and The Dirt', is a continuation of her first story published in the previous anthology in the series, Beyond the Withered Roots, so check out 'Casting in Blood' if you want more from her in this darkly magical world!

About the Publisher - 2023

Becca Barnard was born in Bedford and moved to Wales in 2015. Reading has always been a huge part of her life, from her dad reading The Hobbit to her and her sister before bed, to writing her own fiction (and fanfiction) on Wattpad. She was the first student to achieve a degree in Publishing and Book Culture at Bangor University, and started Barnard Publishing Ltd in response to a lack of publishers in the North, especially in Wales. Also, she hopes one day to join forces with her dad at Barnard Engineering to build Barnard Corp., and one day rule the universe.

Barnard Publishing Ltd was established July 2022 and began trading that following November following the completion of Becca's Masters degree. Bestow These Mortal Roots is the final book in the Roots Trilogy.

For more information about Barnard Publishing, take a look a the resources below;

www.barnardpublishing.co.uk
Barnard.publishing@gmail.com
@Barnardpublishing